C000040259

The Liar

You are holding a reproduction of an original work that is in the public domain in the United States of America, and possibly other countries.You may freely copy and distribute this work as no entity (individual or corporate) has a copyright on the body of the work.This book may contain prior copyright references, and library stamps (as most of these works were scanned from library copies).These have been scanned and retained as part of the historical artifact.

This book may have occasional imperfections such as missing or blurred pages, poor pictures, errant marks, etc. that were either part of the original artifact, or were introduced by the scanning process. We believe this work is culturally important, and despite the imperfections, have elected to bring it back into print as part of our continuing commitment to the preservation of printed works worldwide. We appreciate your understanding of the imperfections in the preservation process, and hope you enjoy this valuable book.

THE LIAR

BY

GILBERT PARKER

AUTHOR OF "THE BATTLE OF THE STRONG,"
"THE SEATS OF THE MIGHTY," ETC.

BOSTON
BROWN AND COMPANY
144 PURCHASE STREET
1899

THE NEW YORK
PUBLIC LIBRARY
224519B

ASTOR, LENOX AND
TILDEN FOUNDATIONS
R   1943   L

Copyright, 1899

BY BROWN AND COMPANY

𝔘𝔫𝔦𝔳𝔢𝔯𝔰𝔦𝔱𝔶 𝔓𝔯𝔢𝔰𝔰

JOHN WILSON AND SON, CAMBRIDGE, U.S.A.

Contents

WOR 19 FEB '36

THE LIAR

CHAPTER I

AN ECHO

"O, de worl' am roun' an' de worl' am wide, —
 O Lord, remember your chillun in de mornin'!
It's a mighty long way up de mountain side,
 An' dey ain't no place whar de sinners kin hide,
 When de Lord comes in de mornin'."

WITH a plaintive quirk of the voice the singer paused, gaily flicked the strings of the banjo, then put her hand flat upon them to stop the vibration, and smiled round on her admirers. The group were applauding heartily: a chorus said: "Another verse, please, Mrs. Detlor."

"Oh, that's all I know, I'm afraid," was the reply. "I haven't sung it for years and years, and I should have to think too hard — no, no, believe me, I can't remember any more. I wish I could, really."

I I

The Liar

A murmur of protest rose, but there came through the window faintly yet clearly a man's voice :

> " Look up and look aroun',
> Fro you' burden on de groun' " —

The brown eyes of the woman grew larger, there ran through her smile a kind of frightened surprise, but she did not start, nor act as if the circumstance were singular.

One of the men in the room — Baron, an honest, blundering fellow — started towards the window to see who the prompter was, but the host — of intuitive perception — saw that this might not be agreeable to their entertainer, and said quietly : " Don't go to the window, Baron. See, Mrs. Detlor is going to sing."

Baron sat down. There was an instant's pause in which George Hagar, the host, felt a strong thrill of excitement. To him Mrs. Detlor seemed in a dream, though her lips still smiled, and her eyes wandered pleasantly over the heads of the company. She was looking at none of them; but her body was bent slightly towards the window, listening with it, as the deaf and dumb do.

Her fingers picked the strings lightly, then warmly, and her voice rose, clear, quaint, and high :

2

An Echo

"Look up an' look aroun',
   Fro you' burden on de groun',
   Reach up an' git de crown,
   When de Lord comes in de mornin' —
   When de Lord comes in de mornin'!"

The voice had that strange pathos, veined with humor, which marks most negro hymns and songs; so that even those present who had never heard an Americanized negro sing, were impressed, and grew almost painfully quiet, till the voice fainted away into silence.

With the last low impulsion, however, the voice from without began again as if in reply. At the first note one of the young girls present made a start for the window. Mrs. Detlor laid a hand upon her arm. "No," she said, "you will spoil — the effect. Let us keep up the mystery."

There was a strange puzzled look on her face, apparent most to George Hagar — the others only saw the lacquer of amusement, summoned for the moment's use.

"Sit down," she added, and she drew the Young Girl to her feet, and passed an arm round her shoulder. This was pleasant to the Young Girl. It singled her out for a notice which would make her friends envious.

3

The Liar

It was not a song coming to them from without, not a melody; but a kind of chant, hummed first in a low, sonorous tone, and then rising and falling in weird undulations. The night was still, and the trees at the window gave forth a sound like the monotonous *s-sh* of rain. The chant continued for about a minute. While it lasted Mrs. Detlor sat motionless, and her hands lay lightly on the shoulders of the Young Girl. Hagar dropped his foot on the floor at marching intervals, — by instinct he had caught at the meaning of the sounds. When the voice had finished Mrs. Detlor raised her head towards the window, with a quick pretty way she had, her eyes much shaded by the long lashes. Her lips were parted in the smile which had made both men and women call her merry, amiable, and fascinating.

"You don't know what it is, of course," she said, looking round, as though the occurrence had been ordinary. "It is a chant hummed by the negro wood-cutters of Louisiana, as they tramp homewards in the evening. It is pretty, is n't it?"

"It's a rum thing," said one they called The Prince, though Alpheus Richmond was the name by which his godmother knew him; "but who's the gentleman behind the scenes — in the green room?"

An Echo

As he said this he looked — or tried to look — knowingly at Mrs. Detlor; for The Prince desired greatly to appear familiar with people and things theatrical; and Mrs. Detlor knew many in the actor and artist world.

Mrs. Detlor smiled in his direction, but the smile was not reassuring. He was, however, delighted. He almost asked her then and there to ride with him on the morrow: but he remembered that he could drive much better than he could ride; and, in the pause necessary to think the matter out, the chance passed — he could not concentrate himself easily.

"Yes, who *is* it?" said the Young Girl.

"Lord, I'll find out," said the flaring Alpheus, a jewelled hand at his tie as he rose.

But their host had made up his mind. He did not know whether Mrs. Detlor did or did not recognize the voice, but he felt that she did not wish the matter to go further. The thing was irregular, if he were a stranger; and if he were not a stranger it lay with Mrs. Detlor whether he should be discovered.

There was a curious stillness in Mrs. Detlor's manner, as though she were waiting further development of the incident. Her mind was in a

5

whirl of memories; there was a strange thumping sensation in her head — yet who was to know that from her manner?

She could not help flashing a look of thanks to Hagar when he stepped quickly between The Prince and the window, and said, in what she called his light comedy manner:

" No, no, Richmond, let us keep up the illusion. The gentleman has done us a service, — otherwise we had lost the best half of Mrs. Detlor's song — we 'll not put him at disadvantage."

" Oh, but look here, Hagar," said the other, protestingly, as he laid his hand upon the curtains.

Few men could resist the quiet decision of Hagar's manner, though he often laughed that having but a poor opinion of his will as he knew it, and believing that he acted firmness without possessing it, save where he was purely selfish. He put his hands in his pockets carelessly, and said in a low decisive tone: " Don't do it, if you please."

But he smiled too, so that others, now gossiping, were unaware that the words were not of as light comedy as the manner. Hagar immediately began a general conversation and asked Baron to sing " The Banks o' Ben Lomond; " feeling sure that Mrs. Detlor did not wish to sing again. Again

6

she sent him a quick look of thanks, and waved her fingers in protest to those who were urging her. She clapped her hands as she saw Baron rise, and the others, for politeness' sake, could not urge her more.

. . . .

For the stranger. Only the morning of that day he had arrived at the pretty town of Herridon among hills and moors, set apart for the idle and ailing of this world. Of the world literally, for there might be seen at the Pump Room visitors from every point of the compass : Hindu gentlemen brought by sons who ate their legal dinners near Temple Bar; invalided officers from Hong Kong, Bombay, Aden, the Gold Coast, and otherwhere; Australian squatters and their daughters; *attachés* of foreign embassies; a Prince from the Straits Settlements; priests without number from the northern counties; Scotch manufacturers; ladies wearied from the London season; artists, actors, and authors, expected to do at inopportune times embarrassing things; and very many from Columbia, Happy Land, who go to Herridon as to Westminster — to see the ruins.

It is difficult for Herridon to take its visitors seriously; and quite as difficult for the visitors to take Herridon seriously. That is what the stranger thought as he tramped back and forth from point to point through the town. He had only been there twelve hours, yet he was familiar with the place. He had the instincts and the methods of the true traveller. He never was guilty of sight-seeing in the usual sense. But it was his habit to get general outlines fixed at once. In Paris, in London, he had taken a map, had gone to some central spot, and had studied the cities from there; had travelled in different directions, merely to get his bearings. After that he was quite at home. This was singular too, for his life had been, of recent years, much out of the beaten tracks of civili-sation! He got the outlines of Herridon in an hour or two, and by evening he could have drawn a pretty accurate chart of it, both as to detail, and from the point of a bird's-eye view at the top of the moor.

The moor had delighted him. He looked away to all quarters, and saw hill and valley wrapped in that green. He saw it under an almost cloud-less sky, and he took off his hat and threw his grizzled head back with a boyish laugh.

"It's good — good enough!" he said. "I've seen so much country all on edge, that this is like

getting a peep over the wall on the other side —
the other side of Jordan. And yet that was God's
country with the sun on it, as Gladney used to say
— poor devil ! "

He dropped his eyes from the prospect before
him, and pushed the sod and ling with his foot
musingly. "If I had been in Gladney's place
would I have done as he did ? and if he had been
in my place would he have done as I did ? One
thing is certain, there 'd have been bad luck for
both of us this way or that, with a woman in the
equation. He was a fool — that 's the way it
looked ; and I was a liar — to all appearances ; and
there 's no heaven on earth for either : I 've seen
that all along the line. One thing is sure : Gladney has reached, as in his engineering phrase he 'd
say, the line of saturation, and I the line of liver,
thanks be to London and its joys ! And now for
sulphur water and — damnation ! "

This last word was not the real end to the sentence. He had, while lighting his cigar, suddenly
remembered something. He puffed the cigar
fiercely, and immediately drew out a letter. He
stood looking at it for a minute, and presently let
go a long breath.

"So much for London, and getting out of my

old tracks! Now, it can't go for another three days, and he needing the dollars. . . . I'll read it over again, anyhow." He took it out and read:

"Cheer up, and get out of the hospital as soon as you can, and come over yourself. And remember in the future that you can't fool about the fire-escapes of a thirteen-story flat, as you can a straight foot-hill of the Rockies, or a Lake Superior silver mine. Here goes to you one thousand dollars (per draft), and please to recall that what's mine is yours, and what's yours is your own, and there's a good big sum that'll be yours: concerning which later. But take care of yourself, Gladney. You can't drown a mountain with a squirt of a rattle-snake's tooth; you can't flood a memory with cognac: I've tried it. For God's sake don't drink any more. What's the use? Smile in the see-saw of the knives. You can only be killed once, and, believe me, there's twice the fun in taking bad luck naked, as it were. Do you remember the time you, and I, and Ned Bassett, the H. B. Company's man, struck the camp of Bloods on the Grey Goose River? how the squaw lied and said he was the trader that dropped their messenger in a hot spring, and they began to *peel* Ned before our eyes? how he said as they drew the first chip from his shoulder: 'Tell the Company, boys, that it's according to the motto on their flag, *Pro Pelle Cutem : Skin for Skin !*' how the woman backed down, and he got off with a strip of his pelt.gone? how the Medicine Man took little bits of us and the red niggers too, and put it on the raw place, and fixed him up again? Well, that's the way to do it; and if you come up smiling every time, you get your pound of flesh one way or another. Play the game with a clear head and a little insolence, Gladney, and you don't find the world so bad at its worst.

"So much for so much. Now for the commission you gave me. I'd rather it had been anything else, for I think I'm the last man in the world for duty where women are concerned. That reads queer, but you know what I mean. I mean that women puzzle me, and I'm apt to take them too literally. If I found your wife, and she wasn't as straightforward as you are, Jack Gladney, I'd as like as not get things in a tangle. You know I thought it would be better to let things sleep — resurrections are uncomfortable things mostly. However, here I am to do what's possible. What have I done? Nothing. I haven't found her yet. You didn't want me to advertise, and I haven't. She hasn't been acting for a long time, and no one seems to know exactly where she is. She was travelling abroad with some people called Branscombes, and I'm going to send a letter through their agent. We shall see.

"Lastly: for business. I've floated the Aurora Company with a capital of a million dollars; and that ought to carry the thing for all we want to do. So, be joyful. But you shall have full particulars next mail. I'm just off to Herridon for the waters. Can you think it, Gladney — Mark Telford, late of the H. B. C., coming down to that? But it's a fact. Luncheons and dinners in London, E. C., with liquids various, have done their fiery work, and so it's stand by the halliards for bad weather! Once more, keep your nose up to the wind, and believe that I am always," etc.

He read it through, dwelling here and there as if to reconsider; and, when it was finished, put it back into his pocket, tore up the envelope, and let it fall to the ground. Presently he said: "I'll cable the money over, and send the letter on next mail. Strange that I did n't think of cabling yesterday. However, it's all the same!"

So saying he came down the moor into the town, and sent his cable; then went to his hotel and had dinner. After dinner he again went for a walk.

An Echo

He was thinking hard, and that did not render him less interesting. He was tall and muscular, yet not heavy, with a lean dark face, keen steady eyes, and dignified walk. He wore a black soft-felt hat and a red silk sash which just peeped from beneath his waistcoat — in all, striking yet not bizarre, and notably of gentleman-like manner. What arrested attention most, however, was his voice. People who heard it invariably turned to look, or listened from sheer pleasure. It was of such penetrating clearness that if he spoke in an ordinary tone it carried far. Among the Indians of the Hudson's Bay Company, where he had been for six years or more, he had been known as Man-of-the-gold-throat; and that long before he was called by the negroes on his father's plantation in the Southern States "Little Marse Gabriel," because Gabriel's horn, they thought, must be like his voice — " only mo' so; an' dat chile was bawn to ride on de Golden Mule."

You would not, from his manner, or voice, or dress, have called him an American. You might have said he was a gentleman planter from Cuba, or Java, or Fiji; or a successful miner from Central America, who had more than a touch of Spanish blood in his veins. He was not at all the

13

type from over sea who are in evidence at Wild West shows, or as poets from a Western Ilion, ride in the Row with sombrero, cloak, and Mexican saddle. Indeed, a certain officer of Indian infantry, who had once picked up some irregular French in Egypt, and at dinner made remarks on Telford's personal appearance to a pretty girl beside him, was confused when Telford looked up and said to him in admirable French, "I 'd rather not, but I can't help hearing what you say; and I think it only fair to tell you so. These grapes are good : shall I pass them ? Poole made my clothes and Lincoln is my hatter. Were you ever in Paris?"

The slow distinct voice came floating across the little table, and ladies who that day had been reading the last French novel, and could interpret every word and tone, smiled slyly at each other, or held themselves still to hear the sequel; the ill-bred turned round and stared; the parvenu sitting at the head of the table, who had been a foreign buyer of some London firm, chuckled coarsely and winked at the waiter; and Baron, the Afrikander trader, who sat next to Telford, ordered champagne on the strength of it. The bronzed, weather-worn face of Telford showed imperturbable, but his eyes were struggling with a strong kind of humor.

An Echo

The officer flushed to the hair, accepted the grapes, smiled foolishly, and acknowledged — swallowing the reflection on his accent — that he had been in Paris. Then he engaged in close conversation with the young lady beside him, who, however, seemed occupied with Telford. This quiet, keen young lady, Miss Mildred Margrave, had received an impression, not of the kind which her sex confide to each other, but of a graver quality. She was a girl of sympathies and parts.

The event increased the interest and respect felt in the hotel for this stranger. That he knew French was not strange. He had been well educated as a boy, and had had his hour with the classics. His godmother, who had been in the household of Prince Joseph Bonaparte, taught him French from the time he could lisp, and, what was dangerous in his father's eyes, filled him with bits of poetry and fine language, so that he knew Heine, Racine, and Beranger, and many another. But this was made endurable to the father by the fact that, by nature, the boy was a warrior and a scapegrace, could use his fists as well as his tongue, and posed as a Napoleon with the negro children on the plantation. He was leader of the revels when the slaves gathered at night in front of the huts, and made a joy of captivity, and sang hymns which sounded like profane music-hall songs, and songs with an unction now lost to the world, even as Shakespere's fools are lost — that gallant company who ran a thread of tragedy through all their jesting.

Great things had been prophesied for this youth in the days when he sat upon an empty treacle barrel with a long willow rod in his hand, a cocked hat on his head, a sword at his side — a real sword once belonging to a little Bonaparte — and fiddlers and banjoists beneath him. His father on such occasions called him Young King Cole.

All had changed, and many things had happened, as we shall see. But one thing was clear: this was no wild man from the West. He had claims to be considered, and he was considered. People watched him as he went down over the esplanade and into quiet streets. The little occurrence at the dinner-table had set him upon a train of thought which he had tried to avoid for many years. On principle he would not dwell on the past: there was no corrosion, he said to himself, like the memory of an ugly deed. But the experiences of the last few days had tended to throw him into the past, and for once he gave himself up to it.

Presently there came to him the sound of a

banjo — not an unusual thing at Herridon. It had its mock negro minstrels, whom, hearing, Telford was anxious to offend. This banjo, he knew at once, was touched by fingers which felt them as if born on them; and the chords were such as are only brought forth by those who have learned them to melodies of the South. He stopped before the house and leaned upon the fence. He heard the voice go silvering through a negro hymn, which was among the first he had ever known. He felt himself suddenly shiver — a thrill of nervous sympathy. His face went hot, and his hands closed on the palings tightly. He stole into the garden quietly, came near the window, and stood still. He held his mouth in his palm; he had an inclination to cry out.

"Good God," he said in a whisper, "to hear that off here after all these years!" Suddenly the voice stopped. There was a murmur within. It came to him indistinctly. "She has forgotten the rest," he said. Instantly, and almost involuntarily, he sang:

> "Look up and look aroun'
> Fro you' burden on de groun'."

Then came the sequel as we described, and his low chanting of the negro wood-cutters' chant.

The Liar

He knew that any who answered it must have lived the life he once lived in Louisiana; for he had never heard it since he had left there, nor any there hum it except those who knew the negroes well. Of an evening, in the hot, placid South, he had listened to it come floating over the sugar-cane and through the brake, and go creeping weirdly under the magnolia trees. He waited, hoping, almost wildly — he knew it was a wild hope — that there would be a reply. There was none. But presently there came to him the Baron's crude, honest singing :

" For you 'll take the high road, and I 'll take the low road,
And I 'll be in Scotland before you :
But I and my true love will never meet again
On the bonnie bonnie banks o' Ben Lomond."

Telford drew in his breath sharply, caught his moustache between his teeth savagely for a minute, then let it go with a run of ironical laughter. He looked round him. He saw in the road two or three people who had been attracted by the music. They seemed so curious merely, so apathetic — his feelings were playing at full tide. To him they were the idle, intrusive spectators of his trouble. All else was dark about him, save where, on the hill, the lights of the Tempe Hotel showed, and a man and woman, his arm round her, could be seen pacing among the trees. Telford turned away from this, ground his heel into the turf, and said: "I wish I could see who she is! *Her* voice? — it's impossible." He edged close to the window, where a light showed at the edge of the curtains. Suddenly he pulled up.

"No, whoever she is I shall know in time. Things come round. It's almost uncanny as it stands; but then, it was uncanny — it has all been so, since the start." He turned to the window again, raised his hat to it, walked quickly out into the road, and made his way to the View Hotel. As he came upon the verandah Mildred Margrave passed him. He saw the shy look of interest in her face, and with simple courtesy he raised his hat. She bowed and went on. He turned and looked after, then, shaking his head as if to dismiss an unreasonable thought, entered, and went to his room.

About this time the party at Hagar's rooms was breaking up. There had been more singing by Mrs. Detlor. She ransacked her memory for half-remembered melodies — whimsical, arcadian, sad, and Hagar sat watching her, outwardly quiet and appreciative, inwardly under an influence like

none he had ever felt before. When his guests
were ready he went with them to their hotel. He
saw that Mrs. Detlor shrank from the attendance
of The Prince, who insisted on talking of the
"stranger in the green-room." When they arrived at the hotel he managed, simply enough, to
send the lad on some mission for Mrs. Detlor,
which, he was determined, should be permanent so
far as that evening was concerned. He was soon
walking alone with her on the terrace. He did
not force the conversation, nor try to lead it to
the event of the evening, which, he felt, was
more important than others guessed. He knew
also that she did not care to talk just then. He
had never had any difficulty in conversation with
her — they had a singular *rapport*. He had travelled much, seen more, remembered everything,
was shy to austerity with people who did not
interest him, spontaneous with those that did, and
yet was never — save to serve a necessary purpose — hail-fellow with any one. He knew that
he could be perfectly natural with this woman,
say anything that became a man. He was an
artist without affectations, a diplomatic man having great enthusiasms and some outer cynicism.
He had started life terribly in earnest before the

world. He had changed all that. In society he
was a nervous organism gone cold, a deliberate,
self-contained man. But in so much as he was
chastened of enthusiasms outwardly, he was boy-
ishly earnest inwardly.

He was telling Mrs. Detlor of some incident he
had seen in South Africa when sketching there
for a London weekly; telling it graphically, incis-
ively — he was not fluent; he etched in speech,
he did not paint. She looked up at him once or
twice, as if some thought was running parallel with
his story. He caught the look. He had just
come to the close of his narrative. Presently she
put out her hand and touched his arm.

"You have great tact," she said, "and I am
grateful."

"I will not question your judgment," he replied
smiling. "I am glad that you think so, and
humbled too."

"Why humbled?" she laughed softly. "I
can't imagine that."

"There are good opinions which make us
vain, others which make us anxious to live up to
them, while we are afraid we can't."

"Few men know that kind of fear. You are
a vain race."

The Liar

"You know best. Men show certain traits to women most."

"That is true. Of the most real things they seldom speak to each other; but to women they often speak freely, and it makes one shudder — till one knows the world, and gets used to it."

"Why shudder?" He guessed the answer, but he wanted, not from mere curiosity, to hear her say it.

"The business of life they take seriously: money, position — chiefly money. Life itself — home, happiness, the affections, friendship — is an incident, a thing to juggle with."

"I do not know you in this satirical mood," he answered. "I need time to get used to it before I can reply."

"I surprise you? People do not expect me ever to be either serious or — or satirical: only look to me to be amiable and merry — 'Your only jig-maker,' as Hamlet said — a sprightly Columbine. Am I rhetorical?"

"I don't believe you are really satirical, and please don't think me impertinent if I say I do not like your irony. The other character suits you; for, by nature, you are, are you not, both merry and amiable? The rest——"

An Echo

"'The rest is silence'...I can remember when mere living was delightful. I did n't envy the birds. That sounds sentimental to a man, does n't it? But then that is the way a happy girl — a child — feels. I do not envy the birds now, though, I suppose, it is silly for a worldly woman to talk so.

"Whom, then, do you envy?"

There was a warm frank light in her eyes. "I envy the girl I was then."

He looked down at her. She was turning a ring about on her finger abstractedly. He hesitated to reply. He was afraid that he might say something to press a confidence, for which she would be sorry afterwards. She guessed what was passing in his mind.

She reached out as if to touch his arm again, but did not, and said: "I am placing you in an awkward position. Pardon me. It seemed to me for a moment that we were old friends — old and candid friends."

"I wish to be an old and candid friend," he replied firmly. "I honor your frankness."

"I know that," she added hastily. "One is safe — with some men."

"Not with a woman?"

"No woman is safe in any confidence to any other woman. All women are more or less bad at heart."

"I do not believe that as you say it."

"Of course you do not — as I say it; but you know what I mean. Women are creatures of impulse, except those who live mechanically and have lost everything. They become like priests then."

"Like some priests. Yet, with all respect, it is not a confessional I would choose, except the woman was my mother."

There was silence for a moment, and then she abruptly said : "I know you wish to speak of that incident and you hesitate. You need not. Yet this is all I can tell you : whoever the man was he came from Tellaire, the place where I was born."

She paused. He did not look, but he felt that she was moved. He was curious as to human emotions, but not where this woman was concerned.

"There were a few notes in that woodcutters' chant which were added to the traditional form by one whom I knew," she continued.

"You did not recognize the voice?"

"I cannot tell. One fancies things, and it was all twelve years ago."

"It was all twelve years ago," he repeated musingly after her. He was eager to know, yet he would not ask.

"You are a clever artist," she said presently. "You want a subject for a picture. You have told me so. You are ambitious. If you were a dramatist I would give you three acts of a play — the fourth is yet to come : but you shall have a scene to paint, if you think it strong enough."

His eyes flashed. The artist's instinct was alive. In the eyes of the woman was a fire which sent a glow over all her features. In herself she was an inspiration to him, but he had not told her that. "Oh, yes," was his reply, "I want it, if I may paint you in the scene."

"You may paint me in the scene," she said quietly. Then, as if it suddenly came to her that she would be giving a secret into this man's hands, she added, "That is, if you want me for a model merely."

"Mrs. Detlor," he said, "you may trust me on my honor."

She looked at him, not searchingly, but with a clear, honest gaze such as one sees oftenest in the eyes of children, — yet she had seen the duplicities of life backwards — and said calmly, " Yes, I can trust you."

" An artist's subject ought to be sacred to him," he said. " It becomes himself, and then it is n't hard — to be silent."

They walked for a few moments, saying nothing. The terrace was filling with people, so they went upon the verandah and sat down. There were no chairs near them. They were quite at the end.

" Please light a cigar," she said, with a little laugh. " We must not look serious. Assume your light comedy manner as you listen, and I will wear the true Columbine expression. We are under the eyes of the curious."

" Not too much light comedy for me," he said. " I shall look forbidding, lest your admirers bombard us."

They were quiet again.

" This is the story," she said at last, folding her hands before her. — " No, no," she added hastily, " I will not tell you the story, I will try and picture one scene. And when I have finished, tell me if you don't think I have a capital imagination." She drew herself up with a little gesture of mockery. " It is comedy, you know : —

26

An Echo

" Her name was Marion Conquest. She was beautiful — they said that of her then — and young ; only sixteen. She had been very happy, for a man said that he loved her, and she wore his ring on her finger. One day, while she was visiting at a place far from her home, she was happier than usual. She wished to be by herself to wonder how it was that one could be so happy. You see, she was young, and did not think often ; she only lived. She took a horse and rode far away into the woods. She came near a cottage among the trees. She got off her horse and led it. Under a tree she saw a man and a woman. The man's arm was round the woman. A child four or five years old was playing at their feet — at the feet of its father and mother ! . . . The girl came forward and faced the man — the man she had sworn to marry. As I said, his ring was on her finger."

She paused. People were passing near, and she smiled and bowed once or twice ; but Hagar saw that the fire in her eyes had deepened.

" Is it strong enough for your picture ? " she said quietly.

" It is as strong as it is painful. Yet there is beauty in it too : for I see the girl's face."

" You see much in her face, of course, for you

27

look at it as an artist: you see shame, indignation, bitterness — what else ? "

" I see that moment of awe when the girl suddenly became a woman — as the serious day breaks all at once through the haze of morning."

" I know you can paint the picture," she said; " but you have no model for the girl. How shall you imagine her ? "

" I said that I would paint you in the scene," he answered slowly.

" But I am not young as she was, am not — so good to look at."

" I said that I saw beauty in the girl's face : I can only see it through yours."

Her hands clasped tightly before her. Her eyes turned full on him for an instant, then looked away into the dusk. There was silence for a long time now. His cigar burned brightly. People kept passing and repassing on the terrace below them. Their serious silence was noticeable.

" A penny for your thoughts," she said gaily, yet with a kind of wistfulness.

" You would be thrown away at the price."

These were things that she longed yet dreaded to hear. She was not free (at least she dreaded so) to listen to such words.

An Echo

"I am sorry for that girl, God knows!" he added.

"She lived to be always sorry for herself. She was selfish. She could have thrived on happiness. She did not need suffering. She has been merry, gay, but never happy."

"The sequel was sad?"

"Terribly sad."

"Will you tell me — the scene?"

"I will, but not to-night." She drew her hands across her eyes and forehead. "You are not asking merely as the artist now?" She knew the answer, but she wanted to hear it.

"A man who is an artist asks; and he wishes to be a friend to that woman, to do her any service possible."

"Who can tell when she might need befriending?"

He would not question further — she had said all she could, until she knew who the stranger was.

"I must go in," she said; "it is late."

"Tell me one thing. I want it for my picture — as a key to the mind of the girl. What did she say at that painful meeting in the woods — to the man?"

The Liar

Mrs. Detlor looked at him as if she would read him through and through. Presently she drew a ring from her finger slowly and gave it to him, smiling bitterly.

"Read inside. That is what she said."

By the burning end of his cigar he read: "*You told a lie.*"

At another hotel a man sat in a window, looking out on the esplanade. He spoke aloud.

"'You told a lie,' was all she said; and as God's in heaven I've never forgotten I was a liar from that day to this."

CHAPTER II

THE next morning George Hagar was early
at the Pump Room. He found it amusing
to watch the crowds coming and going — earnest
invalids, and that most numerous body of middle-
aged, middle-class people who have no particular
reason for drinking the waters, and whose only
regimen is getting even with their appetites. He
could pick out every order at a glance, he did not
need to wait until he saw the tumblers at their
lips. Now and then a dashing girl came gliding
in, and, though the draught was noxious to her,
drank the stuff off with a neutral look and well-
bred indifference to the distress about her. Or,
in strode the private secretary of some distinguished
being in London, S. W. He invariably carried
his glass to the door, drank it off in languid sips
as he leaned indolently against the masonry, and
capped the event by purchasing a rose for his

button-hole; so making a ceremony, which
smacked of federating the world at a common
public drinking trough, into a little *fête*. Or,
there were the good priests from a turbulent lar-
ruping island, who, with cheeks blushing with
health and plump waistcoat, came ambling, smiling, to their thirty ounces of noisome liquor.
Then, there was Baron, the bronzed, idling, com-
fortable trader from Zanzibar, who, after fifteen
years of hide-and-seek with fever and Arabs and
sudden death — wherewith was all manner of
accident, and sundry profane dealings not intended
for the Times, or Exeter Hall, comes back to
sojourn in quiet " Christom " places, a lamb in
temper, a lion at heart, an honest soul who minds
his own business, is enemy to none but the
malicious, and lives in daily wonder that the wine
he drank the night before gets into trouble with
the waters drunk in the morning. And the days,
weeks, and months go on, but Baron remains,
having seen population after population of water-
drinkers come and go. He was there years ago;
he is there still, coming every year: and he does
not know that George Hagar has hung him at
Burlington House more than once, and he re-
members very well the pretty girl he did not

marry, who also, on one occasion, joined the aristocratic company " on the line."

This young and pretty girl — Miss Mildred Margrave — came and went this morning ; and a peculiar, meditative look on her face, suggesting some recent experience, caused the artist to transfer her to his note-book. Her step was sprightly, her face warm and cheerful in hue, her figure excellent, her walk the most admirable thing about her — swaying, graceful, lissome — like perfect dancing : with the whole body. Her walk was immediately merged into somebody else's — merged melodiously, if one may say so. A man came from the pump-room looking after the girl, and Hagar remarked a similar swaying impulsion in the walk of both. He walked as far as the gate of the pump-room, then sauntered back, unfolded a newspaper, closed it up again, lit a cigar, and, like Hagar, stood watching the crowd abstractedly. He was an outstanding figure. Ladies, as they waited, occasionally looked at him through their glasses, and the Duchess of Brevoort thought he would make a picturesque figure for a reception — she was not less sure because his manner was neither savage nor suburban. George Hagar was known to some people as " the fellow who looks back of you;" Mark Telford might have been spoken of as "the man who looks through you;" for, when he did glance at a man or woman, it was with keen directness, affecting the person looked at like a flash of light to the eye. It is easy to write such things, not so easy to verify them; but any one that has seen the sleuthlike eyes of men accustomed to dealing with danger in the shape of wild beasts, or treacherous tribes, or still more treacherous companions, and whose lives depend upon their feeling for peril, and their unerring vigilance — can see what George Hagar saw in Mark Telford's looks.

Telford's glance went round the crowd, appearing to rest for an instant on every person, and for a longer time on Hagar. The eyes of the two men met. Both were immediately puzzled, for each had a sensation of some subterranean origin. Telford immediately afterwards passed out of the gate and went towards the St. Cloud Gardens, where the band was playing. For a time Hagar did not stir, but idled with his pencil and notebook. Suddenly he started, and hurried out in the direction Telford had gone.

"I was an ass," he said to himself, "not to think of that at first."

The Meeting

He entered the St. Cloud Gardens and walked round the promenade a few times, but without finding him. Presently, however, Alpheus Richmond, whose beautiful and brilliant waistcoat, and brass buttons with monogram adorned, showed advantageously in the morning sunshine, said to him : " I say, Hagar, who's that chap up there filling the door of the summer-house ? Lord, rather! "

It was Telford. Hagar wished for the slightest pretext to go up the unfrequented side path and speak to him ; but his mind was too excited to do the thing naturally without a stout pretext. Besides, though he admired the man's proportions, and his uses from an artistic standpoint, he did not like him personally, and he said that he never could. He had instinctive likes and dislikes. What had startled him at the pump-room, and had made him come to the gardens, was the conviction that this was the man to play the part in the scene which, described by Mrs. Detlor, had been arranging itself in a hundred ways in his brain, — the central figures always the same, the details, light, tone, coloring, expression, fusing, resolving. Then came another and still more significant thought. On this he had acted.

The Liar

When he had got rid of Richmond, who begged
that he would teach him how to arrange a tie as
he did, — for which an hour was appointed, —
he determined, at all hazards, to speak. He had
a cigar in his pocket, and though to smoke in the
morning was pain and grief to him, he determined
to ask for a match; and started. He was stopped
by Baron, whose thoughts being much with the
little vices of man, anticipated his wishes, and
offered him a light. In despair, Hagar took it,
and asked if he chanced to know who the stranger
was. Baron did know, assuring Hagar that he
sat on the gentleman's right at the same table
in his hotel, and was qualified to introduce him.
Before they started he told the artist of the occurrence of the evening before, and further assured him
of the graces of Miss Mildred Margrave. "A
pearl," he said, "not to be reckoned by loads of
ivory, nor jolly bricks of gold, nor caravans of
Arab steeds, nor — come and have dinner with me
to-night, and you shall see. There, what do you
say ? "

Hagar, who loved the man's unique and spontaneous character, as only an artist can love a
subject in which he sees royal possibilities, con-
sented gladly, and dropped a cordial hand on the

36

The Meeting

other's shoulder. The hand was dragged down and wrenched back and forth with a sturdy clasp, in time to a roll of round unctuous laughter. Then Baron took him up hurriedly, and introduced him to Telford, with the words: " You two ought to know each other. Telford, traveller, officer of the Hudson's Bay Company, et cetera; Hagar, artist, good fellow, et cetera."

Then he drew back and smiled as the two men, not shaking hands as he expected, bowed, and said they were happy to meet. The talk began with the remark by Hagar on the panorama below them, " that the thing was amusing if not seen too often; but the eternal paddling round the band-stand was too much like marionettes."

" You prefer a Punch and Judy to marionettes ? " asked Telford.

" Yes, you get a human element in a Punch and Judy tragedy. Besides, it has surprises, according to the idiosyncracy of the man in the green room." He smiled immediately, remembering that his last words plagiarized Mr. Alpheus Richmond.

" I never miss a Punch and Judy if I'm near it," said Telford. " I enjoy the sardonic humor with which Punch hustles off his victims. His light-heartedness when doing bloody deeds is the true temper."

"That is, if it must be done, to do it with a grin is — "

"Is the most absolute tragedy."

Hagar was astonished, for even the trader's information that Telford spoke excellent French, and had certainly been a deal on red carpet in his time, did not prepare him for the sharply-incisive words just uttered. Yet it was not incongruous with Telford's appearance — not even with the red sash peeping at the edge of his waistcoat.

They came down among the promenaders, and Baron being accosted by some one, he left the two together, exacting anew the promise from Hagar regarding dinner.

Presently Hagar looked up, and said abruptly : "You were singing outside my window last night."

Telford's face was turned away from him when he began. It came slowly towards him. The eyes closed steadily with his : there was no excitement, only cold alertness.

"Indeed ? What was I singing ? "

"For one thing, the chant of the negro wood-cutters of Louisiana."

The Meeting

" What part of Louisiana ? "

" The county of Tellavie chiefly."

Telford drew a long breath, as though some suspense was over, and then said : " How did you know it was I ? "

"I could scarcely tell you. I got the impression — besides, you are the only man I 've seen in Herridon who looks likely to know it and the song which you prompted."

" Do I look like a Southerner — still ? You see I 've been in an arctic country five years."

" It is not quite that. I confess I cannot explain it."

" I hope you did not think the thing too boorish to be pardoned. On the face of it, it was rude to you — and the lady also."

" The circumstance — the coincidence — was so unusual that I did not stop to think of manners."

" The coincidence — what coincidence ? " said Telford, watching intently.

But Hagar had himself well in hand. He showed nothing of his suspicions. " That you should be there listening, and that the song should be one which no two people, meeting casually, were likely to know."

" We did not meet," said Telford drily.

The Liar

They watched the crowd for a minute. Presently he added : " May I ask the name of the lady who was singing ? "

There was a slight pause, then : " Certainly : Mrs. Fairfax Detlor."

Though Telford did not stir a muscle, the bronze of his face went grayish, and he looked straight before him without speaking. At last he said in a clear, steady voice : " I knew her once, I think."

" I guessed so."

" Indeed ? — May I ask if Mrs. Detlor recognized my voice ? "

" That I do not know; but the chances are she did not, if you failed to recognize hers."

There was an almost malicious desire on Hagar's part to play upon this man — this scoundrel, as he believed him to be — and make him wince still more. A score of things to say or do flashed through his mind; but he gave them up instantly, remembering that it was his duty to consider Mrs. Detlor before all. But he did say : " If you were old friends, you will wish to meet her, of course."

" Yes. I have not seen her in many years. Where is she staying ? "

The Meeting

"At the Tempe Hotel. I do not know whether you intend to call, but I would suggest your not doing so to-day, — that is, if you wish to see her and not merely leave your card, — because she has an engagement this morning, and this afternoon she is going on an excursion."

"Thank you for the generous information." There was cool irony in the tone. "You are tolerably well posted as to Mrs. Detlor's movements."

"Oh, yes," was the equally cool reply. "In this case, I happen to know; because Mrs. Detlor sits for a picture at my studio this morning, and I am one of the party for the excursion."

"Just so. Then will you please say nothing to Mrs. Detlor about having met me? I should prefer surprising her."

"I 'm afraid I can make no promise: the reason is not sufficient. Surprises, as you remarked about Punch and Judy, are amusing, but they may also be tragical."

Telford flashed a dark inquiring look at his companion, and then said: "Excuse me, I did not say that, though it was said. However, it is no matter. We meet at dinner, I suppose, this evening. Till then!"

The Liar

He raised his hat with a slight, sweeping motion, — a little mocking excess in the courtesy — and walked away.

As he went, Hagar said after him between his teeth: " By Heaven, you are *that man !* "

These two hated each other at this moment, and they were men of might after their kind. The hatred of the better man was the greater. Nor from a sense of personal wrong, but —

Three hours later Hagar was hard at work in his studio. Only those who knew him intimately could understand him in his present mood. His pale, brooding, yet masculine face was flushed: the blue of his eyes was almost black; his hair, usually in a Roman regularity about his strong brow, was disorderly. He did not know the passage of time; he had had no breakfast; he had read none of his letters, — they lay in a little heap on his mantelpiece, — he was sketching upon the canvas the scene which had possessed him for the past ten or eleven hours. An idea was being born, and it was giving him the distress of bringing forth. Paper after paper he had thrown away, but, at last, he had shaped the idea to please his severe critical instinct, and was now sketching in the expression of the girl's face. His brain was

The Meeting

hot, his face looked tired; but his hand was steady, accurate, and cool — a shapely hand which the sun never browned, and he was a man who loved the sun.

He drew back at last. "Yes; that's it," he said; "it's right, right. His face shall come in later. But the heart of the thing is there."

The last sentence was spoken in a louder tone, so that some one behind him heard. It was Mrs. Detlor. She had, with the young girl who had sat at her feet the evening before, been shown into the outer room, had playfully parted the curtains between the rooms and entered.

She stood for a moment looking at the sketch, fascinated, thrilled. Her eyes filled with tears, then went dry and hot, as she said in a loud whisper, "Yes, the heart of the thing is there."

Hagar turned on her quickly, astonished, eager, his face shining with a look superadded to his artistic excitement.

She put her finger to her lip, and nodded backwards to the other room. He understood. "Yes, I know," he said, "the light-comedy manner." He waved his hand towards the drawing. "But is it not in the right vein?"

"It is painfully, horribly true," she said. She

43

looked from him to the canvas, from the canvas
to him, and then made a little pathetic gesture
with her hands. " What a jest life is ! "

" A game — a wonderful game," he replied,
"and a wicked one, when there is gambling with
human hearts."

Then he turned with her towards the other ,
room. As he passed her to draw aside the curtain,
she touched his arm with the tips of her fingers
so lightly — as she intended — that he did not feel
it. There was a mute confiding tenderness in
the action more telling than any speech. The
woman had had a brilliant, varied, but lonely life.
It must still be lonely, though now the pleasant
vista of a new career kept opening and closing
before her, rendering her days fascinating yet
troubled, her nights full of joyful but uneasy hours.
The game thus far had gone against her; yet she
was popular, merry, and amiable.

She passed composedly into the other room,
Hagar greeted the Young Girl, gave her books
and papers, opened the piano, called for some re-
freshments, and presented both with a rose from a
bunch upon the table. The Young Girl was perfectly happy to be allowed to sit in the courts
without and amuse herself, while the artist and his

The Meeting

admired model should have their hour with pencil and canvas.

The two then went to the studio again, and, leaving the curtain drawn back, Hagar arranged Mrs. Detlor in position, and began his task. He stood looking at the canvas for a time, as though to enter into the spirit of it again; then turned to his model. She was no longer Mrs. Detlor, but his subject; near to him as his canvas and the creatures of his imagination, but as a mere woman in whom he was profoundly interested (that at least) an immeasurable distance from him. He was the artist only now.

It was strange. There grew upon the canvas Mrs. Detlor's face, all the woman of it, just breaking through sweet, awesomely beautiful, girlish features; and though the work was but begun, there was already that luminous tone which artists labor so hard to get, giving to the face a weird, yet charming expression.

For an hour he worked, then he paused. "Would you like to see it?" he said.

She rose eagerly and a little pale. He had now sketched in more distinctly the figure of a man, changed it purposely to look more like Telford. She saw her own face first. It shone out of the

45

canvas. She gave a gasp of pain and admiration. Then she caught sight of Telford's figure, with the face blurred and indistinct.

"Oh!" she said with a shudder, "that — that is like him. How could you know?"

"If that is the man," he said, "I saw him this morning. Is his name Mark Telford?" .

"Yes," she said, and sank into a chair. Presently she sprang to her feet, caught up a brush, and put it into his hand. "Paint in his face. Quick: paint in his face. Put all his wickedness there."

Hagar came close to her. "You hate him?" he said, and took the brush.

She did not answer by word, but shook her head wearily as to some one far off, expressing neither yes nor no.

"Why?" he said quietly — all their words had been in low tones, that they might not be heard — "why do you wear that ring then?"

She looked at her hand with a bitter, pitiful smile. "I wear it in memory of that girl, who died very young" — she pointed to the picture — "and to remind me not to care for anything too much, lest it should prove to be a lie." She nodded softly to the picture. "He and She are both dead; other people wear their faces now."

The Meeting

"Poor woman!" he said in a whisper. Then he turned to the canvas, and, after a moment, filled in from memory the face of Mark Telford, she watching him breathlessly, yet sitting very still.

After some minutes he drew back and looked at it.

She rose and said, "Yes, he was like that, only you have added what I saw at another time. Will you hear the sequel now?"

He turned and motioned her to a seat, then sat down opposite to her.

She spoke sadly. "Why should I tell you? — I do not know, except that it seemed to me you would understand. Yet I hope men like you forget what is best forgotten; and I feel — oh, do you really care to hear it?"

"I love to listen to you."

"That girl was fatherless, brotherless. There was no man with any right to stand her friend at the time — to avenge her — though, God knows, she wished for no revenge — except a distant cousin who had come from England to see her mother and herself — to marry her if he could. She did not know his motives; she believed that he really cared for her; she was young, and she was sorry for his disappointment. When that thing happened" — (her eyes were on the

47

picture, dry and hard) — "he came forward, determined — so he said — to make the deceiver pay for his deceit with his life. It seemed brave, and what a man would do, what a Southerner would do. He was an Englishman, and so it looked still more brave in him. He went to the man's rooms and offered him a chance for his life by a duel. He had brought revolvers. He turned the key in the door, and then laid the pistols he had brought on the table. Without warning the other snatched up a small sword, and stabbed him with it. He managed to get one of the revolvers, fired, and brought the man down. The man was not killed, but it was a long time before he — Mark Telford there — was well again. When he got up, the girl —"

" Poor girl ! "

" When he got up the girl was married to the cousin who had perilled his life for her. It was madness, but it was so."

Here she paused. The silence seemed oppressive. Hagar, divining her thought, got up, went to the archway between the rooms, and asked the Young Girl to play something. It helped him, he said, when he was thinking how to paint. He went back.

Mrs. Detlor continued : " But it was a terrible

mistake. There was a valuable property in England which the cousin knew she could get by proving certain things. The marriage was to him a speculation. When she waked to that — it was a dreadful awakening — she refused to move in the matter. Is there anything more shameful than speculation in flesh and blood — the heart and life of a child ? — he was so much older than she ! Life to her was an hourly pain — you see she was wild with indignation and shame, and alive with a kind of gratitude and reaction when she married him. And her life? Maternity was to her an agony such as comes to few women who suffer and live. If her child — her beautiful, noble child — had lived, she would, perhaps, one day have claimed the property for its sake. This child was her second love and it died — it died."

She drew from her breast a miniature. He reached out, and, first hesitating, she presently gave it into his hand. It was warm — it had lain on her bosom. His hand, generally so steady, trembled. He raised the miniature to his own lips. She reached out her hand, flushing greatly.

" Oh, please, you must not ! " she said.

" Go on, tell me all," he urged, but still held the miniature in his hand for a moment.

"There is little more to tell. He played a part. She came to know how coarse and brutal he was, how utterly depraved.

"At last he went away to Africa — that was three years ago. Word came that he was drowned off the coast of Madagascar, but there is nothing sure, and the woman would not believe that he was dead unless she saw him so, or some one she could trust had seen him buried. Yet people call her a widow — who wears no mourning" (she smiled bitterly) " nor can until — "

Hagar came to his feet. "You have trusted me," he said, " and I will honor your confidence. To the world the story I tell on this canvas shall be my own."

"I like to try and believe," she said, "that there are good men in the world. But I have not done so these many years. Who would think that of me? — I who sing merry songs, and have danced and am gay — how well we wear the mask, some of us! "

"I am sure," he said, " that there are better days coming for you. On my soul I think it!"

"But he is here," she said. "What for? I cannot think there will be anything but misery when he crosses my path."

The Meeting

"That duel," he rejoined, the instinct of fairness natural to an honorable man roused in him; —"did you ever hear more than one side of it?"

"No; yet sometimes I have thought there might be more than one side. Fairfax Detlor was a coward; and whatever that other was," —she nodded to the picture—"he feared no man."

"A minute!" he said. "Let me make a sketch of it."

He got to work immediately. After the first strong outlines she rose, came to him and said, "You know as much of it as I do—I will not stay any longer."

He caught her fingers in his and held them for an instant. "It is brutal of me. I did not stop to think what all this might cost you."

"If you paint a notable picture and gain honor by it, that is enough," she said. "It may make you famous." She smiled a little wistfully. "You are very ambitious, you needed, you said to me once, a simple but powerful subject which you could paint in with some one's life-blood— that sounds more dreadful than it is . . . well! . . . You said you had been successful, but had never had an inspiration—"

" I have one ! "

She shook her head. " Never an inspiration
which had possessed you as you ought to be to
move the public . . . well ? . . . do you think
I have helped you at all ? I wanted so much to
do something for you."

To Hagar's mind there came the remembrance
of the pure woman who, to help an artist, as
poverty-stricken as he was talented, engaged on
the *Capture of Cassandra*, came into his presence
as Lady Godiva passed through the streets of
Coventry, as hushed and as solemn. A sob shook
in his throat — he was of few but strong emotions;
he reached out, took her wrists in his hands, and
held them hard. " I have my inspiration now," he
said; " I know that I can paint my one great
picture. I shall owe all to you. And for my
gratitude, it seems little to say that I love you —
I love you, Marion."

She drew her hands away, turned her head
aside, her face both white and red. " Oh, hush,
you must not say it ! " she said. " You forget;
do not make me fear you and hate myself. . . .
I wanted to be your friend — from the first, to
help you, as I said; be, then, a friend to me, that
I may forgive myself."

The Meeting

" Forgive yourself — for what ?   I wish to God I had the right to proclaim my love — if you would have it, dear — to all the world. . . . And I will know the truth, for I will find your husband, or his grave."

She looked up at him gravely, a great confidence in her eyes.   " I wish you knew how much in earnest I am — in wishing to help you.   Believe me, that is the first thought.   For the rest I am — shall I say it ? — the derelict of a life ; and I can only drift.   You are young, as young almost as I in years, much younger every other way, for I began with tragedy too soon."

At that moment there came a loud knock at the outer door, then a ring, followed by a cheerful voice calling through the window, — " I say, Hagar, are you there ?   Shall I come in or wait on the mat till the slavey arrives. . . . Oh, here she is — *Salaam ! Talofa ! Aloha !* — which is heathen for How-do-you-do, God-bless-you, and All-hail ! "

These remarks were made in the passage from the door through the hall-way into the room.   As Baron entered, Hagar and Mrs. Detlor were just coming from the studio.   Both had ruled their features into stillness.

53

The Liar

Baron stopped short, open-mouthed, confused, when he saw Mrs. Detlor. Hagar, for an instant, attributed this to a reason not in Baron's mind, and was immediately angry. For the man to show embarrassment was an ill compliment to Mrs. Detlor. However, he carried off the situation, and welcomed the Afrikander genially, determining to have the matter out with him in some sarcastic moment later. Baron's hesitation, however, continued. He stammered, and was evidently trying to account for his call by giving some other reason than the real one, which was undoubtedly held back because of Mrs. Detlor's presence. Presently, he brightened up, and said with an attempt to be convincing: "You know that excursion this afternoon, Hagar? Well, don't you think we might ask the chap we met this morning — first-rate fellow — no pleb — picturesque for the box-seat — go down with the ladies — all like him — eh ? "

"I don't see how we can," replied Hagar coolly — Mrs. Detlor turned to the mantelpiece — "we are full up; every seat is occupied — unless I give up my seat to him."

Mrs. Detlor half turned towards them again, listening acutely. She caught Hagar's eyes in the

mirror and saw, to her relief, that he had no
intention of giving up his seat to Mark Telford.
She knew that she must meet this man whom she
had not seen for twelve years. She felt that
he would seek her, though why she could not tell;
but this day she wanted to forget her past, all
things but one, though she might have to put it
away from her ever after. Women have been
known to live a life-time on the joy of one day.
Her eyes fell again on the mantelpiece, on Hagar's
unopened letters. At first her eyes wandered over
the writing on the uttermost envelope mechanically, then a painful recognition came into them.
She had seen that writing before, that slow, sliding
scrawl, unlike any other, never to be mistaken. It
turned her sick. Her fingers ran up to the envelope,
then drew back. She felt for an instant that she
must take it and open it as she stood there. What·
had the writer of that letter to do with George
Hagar? She glanced at the post-mark. It was
South Hampstead. She knew that he lived in
South Hampstead. The voices behind her grew
indistinct, she forgot where she was. She did
not know how long she stood there so, nor that
Baron, feeling, without reason, the necessity for
making conversation, had suddenly turned the talk

upon a collision, just reported, between two vessels in the Channel. He had forgotten their names and where they hailed from — he had only heard of it, had n't read it; but there was great loss of life. She raised her eyes from the letter to the mirror, and caught sight of her own face. It was deadly pale. It suddenly began to waver before her and to grow black. She felt herself swaying, and reached out to save herself. One hand caught the side of the mirror. It was lightly hung. It loosened from the wall, and came away upon her as she wavered. Hagar had seen the action. He sprang forward, caught her, and pushed the mirror back. Her head dropped on his arm.

The Young Girl ran forward with some water as Hagar placed Mrs. Detlor on the sofa. It was only a sudden faintness. The water revived her. Baron stood dumfounded, a picture of helpless anxiety.

" I ought n't to have drivelled about that accident," he said. " I always was a fool."

Mrs. Detlor sat up, pale, but smiling in a wan fashion. " I am all right now," she said. " It was silly of me — let us go, dear," she added to the Young Girl; " I shall be better for the open

air — I have had a headache all morning. . . .
No, please don't accuse yourself, Mr. Baron,
you are not at all to blame."

"I wish that was all the bad news I have,"
said Baron to himself as Hagar showed Mrs.
Detlor to a landau. Mrs. Detlor asked to be
driven to her hotel.

"I shall see you this afternoon at the excursion,
if you are well enough to go?" Hagar said to
her.

"Perhaps," she said with a strange smile.
Then, as she drove away, "You have not read
your letters this morning." He looked after her
for a moment, puzzled by what she said, and by
the expression of her face.

He went back to the house abstractedly. Baron
was sitting in a chair, smoking hard. Neither
man spoke at first. Hagar went over to the
mantel and adjusted the mirror, thinking the while
of Mrs. Detlor's last words. "You have n't
read your letters this morning," he repeated to
himself. He glanced down and saw the letter
which had so startled Mrs. Detlor.

"From Mrs. Gladney!" he said to himself.
He glanced at the other letters. They were
obviously business letters. He was certain Mrs.

Detlor had not touched them, and had, therefore, only seen this one which lay on top. "Could she have meant anything to do with this?" He tapped it upwards with his thumb. "But why, in the name of Heaven, should this affect her? What had she to do with Mrs. Gladney, or Mrs. Gladney with her?"

With his inquiry showing in his eyes he turned round and looked at Baron meditatively, but unconsciously. Baron, misunderstanding the look, said: "Oh, don't mind me. Read your letters. My business 'll keep."

Hagar nodded, was about to open the letter, but paused, went over to the archway, and drew the curtains. Then he opened the letter. The body of it ran:

"DEAR MR. HAGAR, — I have just learned on my return from the Continent with the Branscombes that you are at Herridon. My daughter Mildred, whom you have never seen — and that is strange, we having known each other so long — is staying at the View House there with the Margraves, whom, also, I think, you do not know. I am going down to-morrow, and will introduce you all to each other. May I ask you to call on me there? Once or twice you have done me a great service, and I may prove my gratitude by asking you to do an-

The Meeting

other. Will this frighten you out of Herridon before I come? I hope not, indeed.

"Always gratefully yours,

"IDA GLADNEY."

He thoughtfully folded the letter up, and put it in his pocket. Then he said to Baron "What did you say was the name of the pretty girl at the View House?"

"Mildred, Mildred Margrave — lovely, 'cometh up as a flower,' and all that. You'll see her to-night."

Hagar looked at him debatingly, then said, "You are in love with her, Baron. Isn't it, — forgive me — isn't it a pretty mad handicap?"

Baron ran his hand over his face in an embarrassed fashion, then got up, laughed nervously, but with a brave effort, and replied: "Handicap, my son, handicap? Of course, it's all handicap. But what difference does that make when it strikes you? You can't help it, can you? It's like loading yourself with gold, crossing an ugly river, but you do it. Yes, you do it, just the same."

He spoke with an affected cheerfulness, and dropped a hand on Hagar's shoulder. It was now Hagar's turn. He drew down the hand and

59

wrung it as Baron had wrung his in the morning. "You're a brick, Baron," he said.

"I tell you what, Hagar. I'd like to talk the thing over once with Mrs. Detlor. She's a wise woman, I believe, if ever there was one; sound as the angels, or I'm a Zulu. I fancy she'd give a fellow good advice, eh? — a woman like her, eh?"

To hear Mrs. Detlor praised was as wine and milk to Hagar. He was about to speak, but Baron, whose foible was hurriedly changing from one subject to another, pulled a letter out of his pocket, and said; "But maybe this is of more importance to Mrs. Detlor than my foolishness. I won't ask you to read it. I'll tell you what's in it. But, first, it's supposed, isn't it, that her husband was drowned?"

"Yes, off the coast of Madagascar. But it was never known beyond doubt. The vessel was wrecked, and it was said all hands but two sailors were lost."

"Exactly. But my old friend Meneely writes me from Zanzibar, telling me of a man who got into trouble with Arabs in the interior — there was a woman in it — and was shot but not killed. Meneely brought him to the coast, and put him into hospital, and said he was going to ship him to

The Meeting

England right away, though he thinks he can't live. Meneely further remarks that the man is a bounder. And his name is Fairfax Detlor. Was that her husband's name?"

Hagar had had a blow. Everything seemed to come at once: happiness and defeat all in a moment. There was a grim irony in it. "Yes, that was the name," he said. "Will you leave the telling to me?".

"That's what I came for. You'll do it as it ought to be done; I could n't."

"All right, Baron."

Hagar leaned against the mantel, outwardly unmoved, save for a numb kind of an expression. Baron came awkwardly to him, and spoke with a stumbling kind of friendliness. "Hagar, I wish the Arabs had got him, so help me!"

"For God's sake think what you are saying."

"Of course it does n't sound right to you, and it would n't sound right from you; but I'm a rowdy colonial, and I'm damned if I take it back! — and I like you, Hagar!" and, turning, he hurried out of the house.

Mrs. Detlor had not stayed at the hotel long; but, as soon as she had recovered, went out for a walk. She made her way to the moor. She

wandered about for a half-hour or so, and at last
came to a quiet place where she had been accustomed to sit. As she neared it she saw pieces of
an envelope lying on the ground. Something in
the writing caught her eye. She stopped, picked
up the pieces, and put them together. "Oh,"
she said with misery in her voice, "what does it
all mean? Letters everywhere, like the Writing
on the Wall!"

She recognized the writing as that of Mark Telford. His initials were in the corner. The envelope
was addressed to John Earl Gladney at Trinity
Hospital, New York. She saw a strange tangle of
events. John Earl Gladney was the name of the
man who had married an actress called Ida Folger,
and Ida Folger was the mother of Mark Telford's
child! She had seen the mother in London; she
had also seen the child with the Margraves, who
did not know her origin, but who had taken her
once when her mother was ill, and had afterwards
educated her with their own daughter. What had
Ida Folger to do with George Hagar, the man who
(it was a joy and yet an agony to her) was more
to her than she dared to think? Was this woman
for the second time to play a part — and what
kind of a part — in her life? What was Mark

The Meeting

Telford to John Gladney? The thing was not pleasant to consider. The lines were crossing and recrossing. Trouble must occur somewhere. She sat down quiet and cold. No one could have guessed her mind. She was disciplining herself for shocks. She fought back everything but her courage. She had always had that, but it was easier to exercise it when she lived her life alone — with an empty heart. Now something had come into her life — but she dared not think of it!

And the people of the hotel at her table, a half-hour later, remarked how cheerful and amiable Mrs. Detlor was. But George Hagar saw that through the pretty masquerade there played .a curious restlessness.

That afternoon they went on the excursion to Rivers Abbey — Mrs. Detlor, Hagar, Baron, Richmond, and many others. They were to return by moonlight. Baron did not tell them that a coach from the View Hotel had also gone there earlier, and that Mark Telford and Mildred Margrave with her friends were with it. There was no particular reason why he should.

Mark Telford had gone because he hoped to see Mrs. Detlor without (if he should think it best)

The Liar

being seen by her. Mildred Margrave sat in the seat behind him, he was on the box seat, — and so far gained the confidence of the driver as to induce him to resign the reins into his hands. There was nothing in the way of horses unfamiliar to Telford. As a child he had ridden like a circus-rider and with the fearlessness of an Arab; and his skill had increased with years. This six-in-hand was, as he said, "nuts to Jacko." Mildred was delighted. From the first moment she had seen this man she had been attracted to him, but in a fashion as to gray-headed Mr. Margrave, who sang her praises to everybody — not infrequently to the wide-open ears of Baron. At last she hinted very faintly to the military officer who sat on the box-seat that she envied him, and he gave her his place. Mark Telford would hardly have driven so coolly that afternoon if he had known that his own child was beside him. He told her, however, amusing stories as they went along. Once or twice he turned to look at her. Something familiar in her laugh caught his attention. He could not trace it. He could not tell that it was like a faint echo of his own.

When they reached the park where the old abbey was, Telford detached himself from the rest

64

The Meeting

of the party, and wandered alone through the paths with their many beautiful surprises of water and wood, pretty grottos, rustic bridges, and incomparable turf. He followed the windings of a stream, till, suddenly, he came out into a straight open valley, at the end of which were the massive ruins of the old abbey, with its stern Norman tower. He came on slowly, thinking how strange it was that he, who had spent years in the remotest corners of the world, having for his companions men adventurous as himself, and barbarous tribes, should be here. His life, since the day he left his home in the South, had been sometimes as useless as creditable. However, he was not of such stuff as to spend an hour in useless remorse. He had made his bed, and he had lain on it without grumbling; but he was a man who counted his life backwards: he had no hope for the future. The thought of what he might have been came on him here in spite of himself, associated with the woman — to him always the girl — whose happiness he had wrecked. For, the other woman, the mother of his child, was nothing to him at the time of the discovery. She had accepted the position, and was going away for ever, even as she did go after all was over.

5   65

The Liar

He expected to see the girl he had loved and wronged this day. He had anticipated it with a kind of fierceness; for, if he had wronged her, he felt that he too had been wronged, though he could never, and would never, justify himself. He came down from the pathway and wandered through the long silent cloisters.

There were no visitors about: it was past the usual hour. He came into the old refectory, and the kitchen with its immense chimney, passed in and out of the little chapels, exploring almost mechanically, yet remembering what he saw; and everything was mingled almost grotesquely with three scenes in his life — two of which we know; the other, when his aged father turned from him dying, and would not speak to him. The ancient peace of this place mocked these other scenes and places. He came into the long, unroofed aisle with its battered sides and floor of soft turf, broken only by some memorial brasses over graves. He looked up and saw upon the walls the carved figures of little grinning demons between complacent angels. The association of these with his own thoughts stirred him to laughter — a low, cold laugh which shone on his white teeth.

Outside, a few people were coming towards the

66

abbey, from both parties of excursionists. Hagar and Mrs. Detlor were walking by themselves. Mrs. Detlor was speaking almost breathlessly. " Yes, I recognized the writing. She is nothing, then, to you ? nor has ever been ? "

" Nothing, on my honor! I did her a service once ; she asks me to do another, of which I am as yet ignorant: that is all. Here is her letter."

CHAPTER III

GEORGE HAGAR was the first to move. He turned and looked at Mrs. Detlor. His mind was full of the strangeness of the situation, this man and woman meeting under such circumstances after twelve years, in which no lines of their lives had ever crossed; but he saw, almost unconsciously, that she had dropped his rose. He stooped, picked it up and gave it to her. With a singular coolness — for, though pale, she showed no excitement — she quietly arranged the flower at her throat, still looking at the figure on the platform. A close observer would occasionally have found something cynical, even sinister, in Mark Telford's clear-cut, smoothly-chiselled face; but at the moment when he wheeled slowly and faced these two, there was in it nothing but what was strong, refined, and even noble. His eye, dark and full, was set deep under well-hung brows, and a duskinesss in the flesh round them gave

68

them softness as well as power: withal, there was a melancholy as striking as it was unusual in him.

In spite of herself Mrs. Detlor felt her heart come romping to her throat, for, whatever this man was to her now, he once was her lover. She grew hot to her fingers. As she looked, the air seemed to palpitate round her, and Mark Telford to be standing in its shining hot surf tall and grand. But, on the instant, there came into this lens the picture she had seen in George Hagar's studio that morning. At that moment Mildred Margrave and Baron were entering at the other end of the long, lonely nave. The girl stopped all at once, and pointed towards Telford, as he stood motionless, uncovered. "See," she said, "how fine, how noble he looks!"

Mrs. Detlor turned for an instant and saw her.

Telford had gazed calmly, seriously at Mrs. Detlor, wondering at nothing, possessed by a strange, quieting feeling. There was, for the moment, no thought of right or wrong, misery or disaster, past or future; only — *this is she!* In the wild whistle of Arctic winds he had sworn that he would cease to remember, but her voice ran laughing through them as it did through the blossoms of the locust trees at Tellavie; and he

could not forget. When the mists rose from the
blue lake on a summer plain, the rosy breath of
the sun bearing them up and scattering them like
thistle-down, he said that he would think no more
of her — but, stooping to drink, he saw her face
in the water, as in the hill-spring at Tellavie; and
he could not forget. When he rode swiftly
through the long prairie grass, each pulse afire,
a keen, joyful wind playing on him as he tracked
the buffalo, he said he had forgotten; but he felt
her riding beside him as she had done on the wide
savannas of the South; and he knew that he could
not forget. When he sat before some lodge in a
pleasant village, and was waited on by soft-voiced
Indian maidens, and saw around him the solitary
content of the North, he believed that he had
ceased to think; but, as the maidens danced with
slow monotony and grave, unmelodious voices,
there came in among them an airy, sprightly figure, singing as the streams do over golden pebbles;
and he could not forget. When in those places
where women are beautiful, gracious, and soulless,
he saw that life can be made into mere conven-
tion, and be governed by a code, he said that he
had learned how to forget: but a pale young
figure rose before him with the simple reproach of

falsehood; and he knew that he should always remember.

She stood before him now. Maybe some premonition, some such smother at the heart as Hamlet knew, came to him then, made him almost statue-like in his quiet, and filled his face with a kind of tragical beauty. Hagar saw it and was struck by it. If he had known Jack Gladney and how he worshipped this man he would have understood the cause of the inspiration. It was all the matter of a moment; then Mark Telford stepped down, still uncovered, and came to them. He did not offer his hand, but bowed gravely and said, " I hardly expected to meet you here, Mrs. Detlor, but I am very glad."

He then bowed to Hagar.

Mrs. Detlor bowed as gravely and replied in an enigmatical tone : " One is usually glad to meet one's countrymen in a strange land."

" Quite so," he said; " and it is far from Tellavie."

" It is not so far as it was yesterday," she added.

At that they began to walk towards the garden, leading to the cloisters. Hagar wondered whether Mrs. Detlor wished to be left alone with Telford.

The Liar

As if divining his thought she looked up at him and answered his mute question, following it with another of incalculable gentleness.

Raising his hat he said conventionally enough : "Old friends should have much to say to each other. Will you excuse me?"

Mrs. Detlor instantly replied in as conventional a tone : "But you will not desert me? I shall be hereabouts, and you will take me back to the coach?"

The assurance was given, and the men bowed to each other. Hagar saw a smile play ironically on Telford's face — saw it followed by a steel-like fierceness in the eye. He replied to both in like fashion ; but one would have said the advantage was with Telford — he had the more remarkable personality.

The two were left alone. They passed through the cloisters without a word. Hagar saw the figures disappear down the long vista of groined arches. "I wish to Heaven I could see how this will all end!" he muttered; then joined Baron and Mildred Margrave.

Telford and Mrs. Detlor passed out upon a little bridge spanning the stream, still not speaking. As if by mutual consent they made their

No Other Way

way up the bank and the hillside to the top of a pretty terrace, where was a rustic seat among the trees. When they reached it, he motioned to her to sit. She shook her head, however, and remained standing close to a tree.

"What you wish to say — for I suppose you do wish to say something — will be brief, of course?"

He looked at her almost curiously.

"Have you nothing kind to say to me, after all these years?" he asked quietly.

"What is there to say now more than — then?"

"I cannot prompt you if you have no impulse. Have you none?"

"None at all. You know of what blood we are, we Southerners. We do not change."

"You changed." He knew he ought not to have said that, for he understood what she meant.

"No, I did not change. Is it possible you do not understand? Or did you cease to be a Southerner when you became — "

"When I became a villain?" He smiled ironically. "Excuse me; go on, please."

"I was a girl, a happy girl. You killed me: I did not change. Death is different. . . . But

73

why have you come to speak of this to me? It
was ages ago. Resurrections are a mistake, believe me."

She was composed and deliberate now. Her
nerve had all come back. There had been one
swift wave of the feeling that once flooded her
girl's heart; it had passed, and left her with the
remembrance of her wrongs and the thought of
unhappy years — through all which she had smiled,
at what cost before the world! Come what would,
he should never know that, even now, the man he
once was remained as the memory of a beautiful
dead thing — not this man come to her like a
ghost.

"I always believed you," he answered quietly;
"and I see no reason to change."

"In that case we need say no more," she said,
opening her red parasol, and stepping slightly
forward into the sunshine, as if to go.

There ran into his face a sudden flush. She
was harder, more cruel, than he had thought were
possible to any woman. "Wait," he said angrily,
and put out his hand as if to stop her. "By
Heaven you shall!"

"You are sudden and fierce," she rejoined
coldly. "What do you wish me to say — what I

did not finish ? — that Southerners love altogether
or — hate altogether ? "

His face became like stone. At last, scarce
above a whisper, he said : " Am I to understand
that you hate me ? that nothing can wipe it out ?
no repentance and no remorse ? You never gave
me a chance for a word of explanation or excuse.
You refused to see me. You returned my letter
unopened. But had you asked her — the woman
— the whole truth — "

" If it could make any difference I will ask her
to-morrow."

He did not understand ; he thought she was
speaking ironically.

" You are harder than you know," he said
heavily. " But I *will* speak ; it is for the last
time. Will you hear me ? "

" I do not wish to, but I will not go."

" I had met her five years before there was anything between you and me. She accepted the situation when she understood that I would not
marry her. The child was born. Time went on.
I loved you. I told her, she agreed to go away to
England. I gave her money. The day you found
us together was to have been the last that I should
see of her. The luck was against me. It always

75

has been — in things that I cared for. You sent a man to kill me — "

" No, no, I did not send anyone. I might have killed you — or her — had I been anything more than a child; but I sent no one. You believe that, do you not ? "

For the first time since they had begun to speak she showed a little excitement, but immediately was cold and reserved again.

" I have always believed you," he said again. " The man who is your husband came to kill me — "

" He went to fight you ! " she said, looking at him more intently than she had yet done.

A sardonic smile played for a moment at his lips. He seemed about to speak through it. Presently, however, his eyes half closed, as with a sudden thought, he did not return her gaze, but looked down to where the graves of monks, and abbots, and sinners maybe, were as steps upon the river bank.

" What does it matter ? " he thought. " She hates me." But he said aloud : " Then, as you say, he came to fight me. I hear that he is dead," he added in a tone still more softened. He had not the heart to meet her scorn with scorn. As he said, it did n't matter if she hated him. It would be worth while remembering, when he had gone, that he had been gentle with her, and had spared her the shame of knowing that she had married not only a selfish brute but a coward and would-be assassin as well. He had only heard rumors of her life since he had last seen her, twelve years before; but he knew enough to be sure that she was aware of Fairfax Detlor's true character. She had known less still of his life; for since her marriage she had never set foot in Louisiana, and her mother, while she lived, never mentioned his name, or told her more than that the Telford plantation had been sold for a song. When Hagar had told him that Detlor was dead, a wild kind of hope had leapt up in him, that perhaps she might care for him still, and forgive him, when he had told all. These last few minutes had robbed him of that hope. He did not quarrel with the fact. The game was lost long ago, and it was foolish to have dreamed, for an instant, that the record could be reversed.

Her answer came quickly : " I do not *know* that my husband is dead. It has never been verified."

He was tempted again, but only for an instant. " It is an unfortunate position for you," he replied.

He had intended saying it in a tone of sympathy, but at the moment he saw Hagar looking up towards them from the Abbey, and an involuntary but ulterior meaning crept into the words. He loved, and he could detect love, as he thought. He knew by the look that she swept from Hagar to him that she loved the artist. She was agitated now, and in her agitation began to pull off her glove. For the moment the situation was his.

"I can understand your being wicked," she said keenly, "but not your being cowardly. That is, and was, unpardonable."

"'That *is* and *was*,'" he repeated after her. "When was I cowardly?" He was composed, though there was a low fire in his eyes.

"Then and now."

He understood well. "I, too, was a coward once," he said, looking her steadily in the eyes; "and that was when I hid from a young girl a miserable sin of mine. To have spoken would have been better, for I could but have lost her, as I've lost her now, for ever."

She was moved, but whether it was with pity, or remembrance, or reproach, he did not know, and never asked; for, looking at her ungloved hand, as she passed it over her eyes wearily, he saw the ring he had given her years before. He stepped forward quickly with a half-smothered cry, and caught her fingers. "You wear my ring," he said. "Marion, you wear my ring; you do care for me still!"

She drew her hand away. "No," she said firmly: "no, Mark Telford, I do not care for you. I have worn this ring as a warning to me — my daily crucifixion. Read what is inside it."

She drew it off and handed it to him. He took it and read the words: "*You — told — a — lie.*" This was the bitterest moment in his life: he was only to know one more bitter, and it would come soon. He weighed the ring up and down in his palm, and laughed a dry, crackling laugh.

"Yes," he said, "you have kept the faith — that you hadn't in me — tolerably well. A liar, a coward, and one who strikes from behind — that is it, isn't it? You kept the faith, and I didn't fight the good fight, eh? Well, let it stand so. Will you permit me to keep this ring? The saint needed it to remind her to punish the sinner. The sinner would like to keep it now; for then he would have a hope that the saint would forgive him some day."

The Liar

The bitterness of his tone was merged at last into a strange tenderness and hopelessness.

She did not look at him. She did not wish him to see the tears spring suddenly to her eyes. She brought her voice to a firm quietness. She thought of the woman, Mrs. Gladney, who was coming; of his child, whom he did not recognize. She looked down towards the Abbey. The girl was walking there between old Mr. Margrave and Baron. She had once hated both the woman and the child. She knew that to be true to her blood she ought to hate them always; but there crept into her heart now a strange feeling of pity for both. Perhaps the new interest in her life was driving out hatred. There was something more. The envelope she had found that day on the moor was addressed to that woman's husband, from whom she had been separated — no one knew why — for years. What complication and fresh misery might be here?

"You may keep the ring," she said.

"Thank you," was his reply; and he put in on his finger looking down at it with an enigmatical expression. "And is there nothing more?"

She wilfully misconstrued his question. She took the torn pieces of envelope from her pocket, and handed them to him. "These are yours," she said.

He raised his eyebrows. "Thank you, again. But I do not see their value. One could almost think you were a detective, you are so armed."

"Who is he? What is he to you?" she asked.

"He is an unlucky man, like myself, and my best friend. He helped me out of battle, murder, and sudden death, more than once; and we shared the same blanket times without number."

"Where is he now?" she said in a whisper, not daring to look at him lest she should show how disturbed she was.

"He is in a hospital in New York."

"Has he no friends?"

"Do I count as nothing at all?"

"I mean no others — no wife or family?"

"He has a wife, and she has a daughter; that is all I know. They have been parted — through some cause. Why do you ask? Do you know him?"

"No, I do not know him."

"Do you know the wife? Please tell me; for at his request I am trying to find her, and I have failed."

"Yes, I know her," she said, painfully and slowly. "You need search no longer. She will be at your hotel to-night."

He started, then said : "I'm glad of that. How did you come to know ? Are you friends ? "

Though her face was turned from him resolutely, he saw a flush creep up her neck to her hair.

"We are not friends," she said vaguely. "But I know that she is coming to see her daughter."

"Who is her daughter ? "

She raised her parasol towards the spot where Mildred Margrave stood, and said : "That is her daughter."

"Miss Margrave ? Why has she a different name ? "

"Let Mrs. Gladney explain that to you. Do not make yourself known to the daughter till you see her mother. Believe me, it will be better — for the daughter's sake."

She now turned and looked at him with a pity through which trembled something like a troubled fear. "You asked me to forgive you," she said. "Good-by, — Mark Telford, I do forgive you." She held out her hand. He took it, shaking his head a little over it, but said no word.

No Other Way

"We had better part here, and meet no more," she added.

"Pardon, but banishment," he said, as he let her hand go.

"There is nothing else possible in this world," she rejoined in a muffled voice.

"Nothing, in this world," he replied. "Good-by, till we meet again — somewhere."

So saying he turned and walked rapidly away. Her eyes followed him, a look of misery, horror, and sorrow upon her. When he had disappeared in the trees she sat down on the bench. "It is dreadful," she whispered awe-stricken; "his friend, her husband ; his daughter there, and he does not know her ! What will the end of it be ? "

She was glad she had forgiven him, and glad he had the ring. She had something in her life now that helped to wipe out the past — still, a something of which she dared not think freely. The night before she had sat in her room thinking of the man who was giving her what she had lost many years past, and, as she thought, she felt his arm steal around her and his lips on her cheek; but at that, a mocking voice said in her ear: "You are my wife ; I am not dead ! " And her happy dream was gone.

The Liar

George Hagar, looking up from below, saw her sitting alone, and slowly made his way towards her. The result of the meeting between these two seemed evident : the man had gone. Never in his life had Hagar suffered more than in the past half-hour. That this woman whom he loved — the only woman he had ever loved as a mature man loves — should be alone with the man who had made shipwreck of her best days, set his veins on fire. She had once loved Mark Telford — was it impossible that she should love him again ? He tried to put the thought from him as ungenerous, unmanly, but there is a maggot which gets into men's brains at times, and it works its will in spite of them. He reasoned with himself, he recalled the look of perfect confidence and honesty with which she regarded him before they parted just now. He talked gaily to Baron and Mildred Margrave, told them to what different periods of architecture the ruins belonged, and by sheer force of will drove away a suspicion, a fear, as unreasonable as it was foolish. Yet, as he talked, the remembrance of the news he had to tell Mrs. Detlor, which might (probably would) be shipwreck to his hopes of marriage, came upon him, and presently made him silent, so that he wandered away from the others. He was concerned as to whether he should tell Mrs. Detlor at once what Baron had told him, or hold it till next day, when she might, perhaps, be better prepared to hear it: though he could not help a smile at this, for would not any woman — ought not any woman to ? — be glad that her husband was alive? He would wait. He would see how she had borne the interview with Telford.

Presently he saw that Telford was gone. When he reached her she was sitting, as he had often seen her, perfectly still, her hands folded in her lap upon her parasol, her features held in control, save that in her eyes was a bright hot flame which so many have desired to see in the eyes of those they love, and have not seen. The hunger of these is like the thirst of the people who waited for Moses to strike the rock.

He sat down without speaking. " He is gone," he said at last.

" Yes. Look at me and tell me if, from my face, you would think I had been seeing dreadful things." She smiled sadly at him.

" No, I could not think it: I see nothing more than a kind of sadness — the rest is all beauty."

"Oh, hush!" she replied solemnly; "do not say those things now."

"I will not, if you do not wish to hear them. What dreadful things have you seen?"

"You know so much, you should know everything," she said; "at least, all of what may happen."

Then she told him who Mildred Margrave was; how years before, when the girl's mother was very ill, and it was thought she would die, the Margraves had taken the child and promised that she should be as their own, and a companion to their own child; that their own child had died; and Mildred still remained with them. All this she knew from one who was aware of the circumstances. Then she went on to tell him who Mildred's mother and father were, what were Telford's relations to John Gladney, and of his search for Gladney's wife.

"Now," she said, "you understand all. They must meet!"

"He does not know who she is?"

"He does not. He only knows as yet that she is the daughter of Mrs. Gladney, who, he thinks, is a stranger to him."

"You know his nature; what will he do?"

No Other Way

"I cannot tell. What can he do? — nothing, nothing!"

"You are sorry for him? You —"

"Do not speak of that," she said in a choking whisper. "God gave women pity to keep men from becoming demons. You can pity the executioner when, killing you, he must kill himself next."

"I do not understand you quite; but all you say is wise."

"Do not try to understand it or me, I am not worth it."

"You are worth, God knows, a better, happier fate!"

The words came from him unexpectedly, impulsively. Indirect as they were, she caught a hidden meaning. She put out her hand.

"You have something to tell me. Speak it! Say it quickly! Let me know it now! One more shock more or less cannot matter."

She had an intuition as to what it was. "I warn you, dear," he said, "that it will make a difference, a painful difference, between us."

"No, George" — it was the first time she had called him that — "nothing can make any difference with that."

The Liar

He told her simply, bravely — she was herself so brave — what there was to tell: that two weeks ago her husband was alive, and that he was now on his way to England — perhaps in England itself. She took it with an unnatural quietness. She grew distressingly pale, but that was all. Her hand lay clenched tightly on the seat beside her. He reached out, took it, and pressed it, but she shook her head.

"Please do not sympathize with me," she said. "I cannot bear it. I am not adamant. You are very good — so good to me, that no unhappiness can be all unhappiness. But let us look not one step further into the future."

"What you wish I shall do always."

"Not what I wish, but what you and I ought to do is plain."

"I ask one thing only. I have said that I love you: said it as I shall never say it to another woman — as I never said it before. Say to me once here, before we know what the future will be, that you love me. Then I can bear all."

She turned and looked him full in the eyes, that infinite flame in her own which burns all passions into one: "I cannot — *dear*," she said.

Then she hurriedly rose, her features quivering. Without a word they went down the quiet path to the river, and on towards the gates of the park, where the coach was waiting to take them back to Herridon.

They did not see Mark Telford before their coach left. But, standing back in the shadow of the trees, he saw them. An hour before he had hated Hagar, and had wished that they were in some remote spot alone with pistols in their hands. Now he could watch the two together without anger, almost without bitterness. He had lost in the game, and he was so much the true gamester that he could take his defeat — when he knew it was defeat — quietly. Yet the new defeat was even harder on him than the old. All through the years since he had seen her there had been the vague conviction, under all his determination to forget, that they would meet again, and that all might come right. That was gone, he knew, irrevocably.

" That 's over," he said, as he stood looking at them. "The king is dead : long live the king!"

He lit a cigar and watched the coach drive away ; then saw the coach in which he had come drive up also, and its passengers mount. He did not stir, but smoked on. The driver waited for some time, and when he did not come, drove away without him, to the regret of the passengers and to the indignation of Miss Mildred Margrave, who talked much of him during the drive back.

When they had gone, Telford rose and walked back to the ruined abbey. He went to the spot where he had first seen Mrs. Detlor that day, then took the path up the hillside to the place where they had stood. He took from his pocket the ring she had given back to him, read the words inside it slowly, and, looking at the spot where she had stood, said aloud:

" I met a man once who imagined he was married to the spirit of a woman living at the North Pole. Well, I will marry myself to the ghost of Marion Conquest!"

So saying he slipped the ring on his little finger. The thing was fantastic, but he did it reverently; nor did it appear in the least as weakness, for his face was strong and cold. "Till death us do part —so help me God!" he added.

He turned and wandered once more through the abbey, strayed in the grounds, and at last came to the park gates. Then he walked to the town a couple of miles away, went to the railway station, and took train for Herridon. He arrived there some time before the coach did. He went straight to the View House, proceeded to his room, and sat down to write some letters. Presently he got up, went down to the office, and asked the porter if Mrs. John Gladney had arrived from London. The porter said she had. He then felt in his pocket for a card, but changed his mind, saying to himself that his name would have no meaning for her. He took a piece of letter-paper and wrote on it: "A friend of your husband brings a message to you." He put it in an envelope and, addressing it, sent it up to her. The servant returned, saying that Mrs. Gladney had taken a sitting-room in a house adjacent to the hotel, and was probably there. He took the note and went to the place indicated, sent in the note, and waited.

When Mrs. Gladney received the note she was arranging the few knick-knacks she had brought. She read the note hurriedly, and clenched it in her hand. "It is his writing — his, Mark Telford! — he, my husband's friend! — good God!"

For a moment she trembled violently, and ran her fingers through her golden hair distractedly; but she partly regained her composure, came forward, and told the servant to show him into the room. She was a woman of instant determination. She drew the curtains closer, so that the room would be almost dark to one entering from the sunlight. Then she stood with her back to the light of the window. He saw a figure standing in the shadow, came forward and bowed, not at first looking closely at the face.

"I have come from your husband," he said. "My name is Mark Telford—"

"Yes, I know," she interrupted.

He started, came a little nearer, and looked curiously at her. "Ida—Ida Royal!" he exclaimed. "Are you—you—John Gladney's wife?"

"He is my husband."

Telford folded his arms, and, though pale and haggard, held himself firmly. "I could not have wished this for my worst enemy," he said at last. "Gladney and I have been more than brothers."

"In return for having—"

"Hush!" he interrupted. "Do you think anything you may say can make me feel worse than I do? I tell you we have lain under the same blankets, month in, month out—and he saved my life."

"What is the message you bring?" she asked.

"He begs you to live with him again—you and your child. The property he settled on you for your lifetime he will settle on your child. Until these past few days he was himself poor. To-day he is rich — money got honestly, as you may guess."

"And if I am not willing to be reconciled?"

"There was no condition."

"Do you know all the circumstances — did he tell you?"

"No, he did not tell me. He said that he left you suddenly for a reason; and when he wished to return you would not have him. That was all. He never spoke but kindly of you."

"He was a good man."

"He *is* a good man."

"I will tell you why he left me. He learned, no matter how, that I had not been married, as I said I had."

She looked up, as if expecting him to speak. He said nothing, but stood with eyes fixed on the floor.

"I admitted, too, that I kept alive the memory of a man who had played an evil part in my life; that I believed I cared for him still, more than for my husband."

"Ida! — for God's sake! — you do not mean —— ?"

"Yes, I meant you then. But when he went away, when he proved himself so noble, I changed —I learned to hate the memory of the other man. But he came back too soon. I said things madly, things I did not mean. He went again. And then afterwards I knew that I loved him."

"I am glad of that, upon my soul!" said Telford, letting go a long breath.

She smiled strangely and with a kind of hardness. "A few days ago I had determined to find him if I could, and to that end I intended to ask a man who had proved himself a friend to learn, if possible, where he was in America. I came here to see him — and my daughter."

"Who is the man?"

"Mr. George Hagar."

A strange light shot from Telford's eyes. "Hagar is a fortunate man," he said. Then, dreamily: "You have a daughter. I wish to God that — that ours had lived!"

"You did not seem to care, when I wrote and told you that she was dead."

"I do not think that I cared then. Besides —"

"Besides, you loved that other woman; and my child was nothing to you," she said with low scorn. "I have seen her in London. I am glad

—glad that she hates you. I know she does," she added. "She would never forgive you. She was too good for you; and you ruined her life."

He was very quiet, and spoke in a clear meditative voice: "You are right. I think she hates me. But you are wrong, too, for she has forgiven me."

"You have seen her?" She eyed him sharply.

"Yes, to-day." His look wandered to a table whereon was a photograph of her daughter. He glanced at it keenly. A look of singular excitement sprang to his eyes. "That is your daughter?"

She inclined her head. "How old is she?" He picked up the photograph and held it, scrutinizing it.

"She is seventeen," was the reply in a cold voice.

He turned a worn face from the picture to the woman. "She is my child. You lied to me."

"It made no difference to you then, why should it make any difference now? Why should you take it so tragically?"

"I do not know; but now —?" His head moved, his lips trembled.

"But now she is the daughter of John Gladney's wife. She is loved and cared for by people who

95

are better, infinitely better, than her father and mother were — or could be. She believes her father is dead; and he *is* dead!"

"My child! my child!" he whispered brokenly over the photograph. "You will tell her that her father is not dead; you — "

She interrupted. "Where is that philosophy which you preached to me, Mark Telford, when you said you were going to marry another woman, and told me that we must part? Your child has no father. You shall not tell her. You will go away and never speak to her. Think of the situation. Spare her, if you do not spare me — or your friend John Gladney."

He sat down in a chair, his clenched hands resting on his knees. He did not speak. She could see his shoulder shaking a little, and presently a tear dropped on his cheek.

But she did not stir. She was thinking of her child. "Had you not better go?" she said at last. "My daughter may come at any moment."

He rose and stood before her. "I had it all; and I have lost it all!" he said. "Good-by." He did not offer his hand.

"Good-by. Where are you going?"

"Far enough away to forget," he replied in a

shaking voice. He picked up the photograph, moved his hand over it softly as though he were caressing the girl herself, lifted it to his lips, put it down, and then silently left the room, not looking back.

He went to his rooms, and sat writing for a long time steadily. He did not seem excited or nervous. Once or twice he got up, and walked back and forth, his eyes bent on the floor. He was making calculations regarding the company he had floated in London, and certain other matters. When he had finished writing, three letters lay sealed and stamped upon the table. One was addressed to John Gladney, one to the Hudson's Bay Company, and one to a solicitor in London. There was another unsealed. This he put in his pocket. He took the other letters up, went down stairs, and posted them. Then he asked the hall-porter to order a horse for riding—the best mount in the stables—to be ready at the door in an hour. He again went to his rooms, put on a riding-suit, came down, and walked out across the esplanade and into the street where Hagar's rooms were. They were lighted. He went to the hall door, opened it quietly, and entered the hall. He tapped at the door of Hagar's sitting-room. As he did so a servant came out, and, in reply to a question, said that Mr. Hagar had gone to the Tempe Hotel, and would be back directly. He went in and sat down. The curtains were drawn back between the two rooms. He saw the easels with their backs to the archway. He rose, went in, and looked at the sketches in the dim light.

He started, flushed, and his lips drew back over his teeth with an animal-like fierceness; but immediately he was composed again. He got two candles, brought them, and set them on a stand between the easels. Then he sat down and studied the paintings attentively. He laughed once with a dry recklessness. " This tells her story admirably — he is equal to his subject. To be hung in the Academy — well! well ! "

He heard the outer door open, then immediately Hagar entered the room, and came forward to where he sat. The artist was astonished, and, for the instant, embarrassed. Telford rose. " I took the liberty of waiting for you, and, seeing the pictures, was interested."

Hagar bowed coldly. He waved his hand towards the pictures. " I hope you find them truthful."

"I find them, as I said, interesting. They will make a sensation — and is there anything more necessary? You are a lucky man, and you have the ability to take advantage of it. Yes, I greatly admire your ability — I can do that, at least, though we are enemies, I suppose."

His words were utterly without offence. A melancholy smile played on his lips. Again Hagar bowed, but did not speak.

Telford went on. "We are enemies, and yet I have done you no harm. You have injured me, have insulted me, and yet I do not resent it: which is strange, as my friends in a wilder country would tell you."

Hagar was impressed, affected. "How have I injured you? — by painting these?"

"The injury is this. I loved a woman, and wronged her, but not beyond reparation. Years passed. I saw her, and loved her still. She might still have loved me, but another man came in — it was you. That was one injury. Then — !" He took up a candle and held it to the sketch of the discovery. — "This is perfect in its art and chivalry; it glorifies the girl. That is right." He held the candle above the second sketch. "This," he said, "is admirable as art

99

and fiction. But it is fiction. I have no hope
that you will change it. I think you would make
a mistake to do so. You could not have the situation, if the truth were painted, — your audience
will not have the villain as the injured man."

"Were you the injured man ? "

Telford put the candle in Hagar's hand. Then
he quickly took off his coat, waistcoat, and collar,
and threw back his shirt from his neck behind.

"The bullet-wound I received on that occasion
was in the back," he said. "The other man tried
to play the assassin. Here is the scar. He posed
as the avenger, the hero, and the gentleman; I
was called the coward and the vagabond! He
married the girl."

He started to put on his waistcoat again.
Hagar caught his arm and held it. The clasp
was emotional and friendly. "Will you stand
so for a moment ? " he said. Just so, that I
may— "

"That you may paint in the truth ? No. You
are talking as the man. As an artist you were
wise to stick to your first conception. It had the
heat of inspiration. But I think you can paint me
better than you have done in these sketches.
Come, I will give you a sitting. Get your

brushes. No, no, I'll sit for nothing else than for these scenes, as you have painted them. Don't miss your chance for fame."

Without a word Hagar went to work, and sketched into the second sketch Telford's face as it now was in the candle-light — worn, strong, and with those watchful eyes sunk deep under the powerful brows. The artist in him became greater than the man; he painted in a cruel sinister expression also. At last he paused, his hand trembled. "I can paint no more," he said.

Telford looked at the sketch with a cold smile. "Yes, that's right," he said. "You've painted in a good bit of the devil, too. You owe me something for this; I have helped you to a picture, and have given you a sitting. There is no reason why you should paint the truth to the world. But I ask you this : When you know that *her* husband is dead and she becomes your wife, tell her the truth about that, will you? — how the scoundrel tried to kill me — from behind. I'd like to be cleared of cowardice some time. You can afford to do it. She loves you. You will have everything; I nothing — nothing at all."

There was a note so thrilling, a golden *timbre* to the voice, an indescribable melancholy, so affecting

that Hagar grasped the other's hand and said:
"So help me God, I will!"

"All right."

He prepared to go. At the door Hagar said to
him: "Shall I see you again?"

"Probably — in the morning. Good-night."

Telford went back to the hotel and found the
horse he had ordered at the door. He got up at
once. People looked at him curiously, it was
peculiar to see a man riding at night — for pleasure — and, of course, it could be for no other
purpose. "When will you be back, sir?" said
the groom.

"I do not know." He slipped a coin into the
groom's hand. "Sit up for me. The beast is a
good one?"

"The best we have. Been a hunter, sir."

Telford nodded, stroked the horse's neck, and
started. He rode down towards the gate. He
saw Mildred Margrave coming towards him.

"Oh, Mr. Telford," she said, "you forsook us
to-day, which was unkind. Mamma says — she
has seen you, she tells me — that you are a friend
of my step-father, Mr. Gladney. That's nice, for
I like you ever so much, you know." She raised
her warm, intelligent eyes to his. "I've felt since

you came yesterday that I'd seen you before; but mamma says that's impossible. And it is, I suppose, is n't it? You don't remember me?"

" I *did n't* remember you," he said.

" I wish I were going for a ride, too, in the moonlight — I mean mamma, and I, and you. You ride as well as you drive, of course."

" I wish you were going with me," he replied. He suddenly reached down his hand. "Goodnight." Her hand was swallowed in his firm clasp for a moment. " God bless you, dear," he added, then raised his hat quickly, and was gone.

" I must have reminded him of some one," the girl said to herself. " He said ' God bless you, dear ! ' "

About that time Mrs. Detlor received a telegram from the doctor of a London hospital. It ran : —

" Your husband here. Was badly injured in a channel collision last night. Wishes to see you."

There was a train leaving for London a half-hour later. She made ready hastily, enclosed the telegram in an envelope addressed to George Hagar, and, when she was starting, sent it over to his rooms. When he received it he caught up a time-table, saw that a train would leave in a few minutes, ran out, but could not get a cab quickly, and arrived at the station only to see the train drawing away. " Perhaps it is better so," he said, " for her sake."

That night the solitary roads about Herridon were travelled by a solitary horseman, riding hard. Mark Telford's first ambition when a child was to ride a horse. As a man he liked horses almost better than men. The cool, stirring rush of wind on his face as he rode was the keenest of delights. He was enjoying the ride with an iron kind of humour. For there was in his thought a picture — " The sequel's sequel for Hagar's brush to-morrow," he said, as he paused on the top of a hill, to which he had come from the high road, and looked round upon the verdant valleys, almost spectrally quiet in the moonlight. He got off his horse, and took out a revolver. It clicked in his hand.

" No," he said, putting it up again, " not here. It would be too damned rough on the horse, after riding so hard, to leave him out all night ! "

He mounted again. He saw before him a fine stretch of moor at an easy ascent. He pushed the horse on, taking a hedge or two as he went. The animal came over the highest point of the hill at full speed. Its blood was up, like its

master's.   The hill below this point suddenly
ended in a quarry.   Neither horse nor man knew
it, until the yielding air cried over their heads like
water over a drowning man, as they fell to the
rocky bed far beneath.

An hour after Telford became conscious.   The
horse was breathing painfully and groaning beside
him.   With his unbroken arm he felt for his
revolver — it took him a long time.

"Poor beast," he said, and pushed the hand out
towards the horse's head.   In an instant the
animal was dead.

He then drew the revolver to his own temple,
but paused.   "No, it was n't to be," he said,
"I 'm a dead man, anyway!" and fell back.

Day was breaking when the agony ceased.   He
felt the gray damp light on his eyes, though he could
not see.   He half raised his head.   "God — bless
— you, dear!" he said.   And that ended it.

He was found by the workers at the quarry.   In
Herridon to this day — it all happened years ago —
they speak of the Hudson's Bay Company's man
who made that terrible leap, and, broken all to
pieces himself, had heart enough to put his horse
out of misery.   The story went about so quickly,
and so much interest was excited because the

The Liar

Hudson's Bay Company sent an officer down to bury him, and the new-formed Aurora Company was represented by two or three titled directors, that Mark Telford's body was followed to its grave by hundreds of people. It was never known to the public that he had contemplated suicide. Only John Gladney and the Hudson's Bay Company knew that for certain.

The will, found in his pocket, left everything he owned to Mildred Margrave — that is, his interest in the Aurora Mines of Lake Superior, which pay a gallant dividend. The girl did not understand why this was, but supposed it was because he was a friend of John Gladney, her step-father, and perhaps (but this she never said) because she reminded him of some one. Both she and John Gladney, when they are in England, go once a year to Herridon, and they are constantly sending flowers there.

Alpheus Richmond showed respect for him by wearing a silk sash under his waistcoat, and Baron by purchasing shares in the Aurora Company.

When Mark Telford lay dead, George Hagar tried to take from his finger the ring which carried the tale of his life and death inside it; but the hand was clenched so that it could not be opened.

No Other Way

Two years afterwards, when he had won his fame through two pictures called *The Discovery* and *The Sequel*, he told his newly-married wife of this. And he also cleared Mark Telford's name of cowardice in her sight, for which she was grateful.

It is possible that John Gladney and George Hagar understood Mark Telford better than the woman who once loved him. At least they think so.

The Red Patrol

✿

ST. AUGUSTINE'S, Canterbury, had given
him its licentiate's hood, the Bishop of Ru-
pert's Land had ordained him, and the North had
swallowed him. He had gone forth with his surplice, stole, hood, a sermon-case, the prayer-book
and that Other. Indian camps, trappers' huts,
and Hudson's Bay Company's posts had given
him hospitality and had heard him with patience
and consideration. At first he wore the surplice,
stole and hood, took the eastward position, and
intoned the service, and no man said him nay,
but looked curiously and was sorrowful — he was
so youthful, clear of eye, and bent on doing heroic
things. But little by little there came a change.
The hood was left behind at Fort O'Glory, where
it provoked the derision of the Methodist missionary who followed him, the sermon-case stayed at

The Red Patrol

Fort O'Battle, and at last the surplice itself at the
H. B. C. post at Yellow Quill. He was too
excited and in earnest at first to see the effect of
his ministrations, but there came slowly over him
the knowledge that he was talking into space.
He felt something returning on him out of the air
into which he talked, and buffeting him. It was
the Spirit of the North, in which lives the awful
natural, the large heart of things, the soul of the
past. He awoke to his inadequacy, to the fact that
all these men to whom he talked, listened, and
only listened, and treated him with a gentleness
which was almost pity — as one might a woman.
He had talked doctrine, the Church, the sacra-
ments ; and at Fort O'Battle he awoke to the
futility of his work. What was to blame: the
Church — religion — himself?

It was at Fort O'Battle he met Pretty Pierre,
and there that he heard a voice say over his
shoulder as he walked out into the icy evening,
" *The voice of one crying in the wilderness . . .
and he had sackcloth about his loins, and his food was
locusts and wild honey.*"

He turned to see Pierre, who in the large room
of the post had sat and watched him as he prayed
and preached. He remembered the keen curious

eye, the musing look, the habitual disdain at the lips. It had all touched him, confused him. And now he had a kind of anger.

"You know it so well, why don't you preach yourself?" he said feverishly.

"I have been preaching all my life," Pierre answered dryly.

"The devil's game: cards and law-breaking, and you sneer at men who try to bring lost sheep into the fold."

"The fold of the Church — yes, I understand all that," Pierre answered. "I have heard you and the priests of my father's Church say that. Which is right? But as for me, I am a missionary. I have preached. Cards, law-breaking — these are what I have done. But these are not what I have preached."

"What have you preached?" asked the other, walking on into the fast-gathering night, beyond the post and the Indian lodges into the wastes where frost and silence lived.

Pierre waved his hand towards space. "This," he said.

"What's *this*?" asked the other fretfully.

"The thing you feel round you here."

"I feel the cold," was the petulant reply.

The Red Patrol

"I feel the Immense, the Far Off," said Pierre, slowly.

The other did not understand as yet. "You've learnt big words," he said.

"No, big things," rejoined Pierre, sharply — "a few."

"Let me hear you preach them," half snarled Sherburne.

"You will not like to hear them — no."

"I'm not likely to think about them one way or another," was the contemptuous reply.

Pierre's eyes half closed. The young, impetuous, half-baked college man, to set his little knowledge against his own studious vagabondage! At that instant he determined to play a game and win; to turn this man into a vagabond also, to see John the Baptist become a Bedouin. He saw the doubt, the uncertainty, the shattered vanity in the youth's mind, the missionary's half-retreat from his cause. A crisis was at hand. The youth was fretful with his great theme, instead of being severe upon himself. For days and days Pierre's presence had acted on him silently, but forcibly. He had listened to the vagabond's philosophy, and knew that it was of a deeper — so much deeper — knowledge of life than he himself possessed, and he knew also that it was terribly true—he was not wise enough to see it was only true in part. The influence had been insidious, delicate, cunning, and he himself was only "a voice crying in the wilderness," without the simple creed of that voice. He knew that the Methodist missionary was believed in more, and less liked than himself.

Pierre would work now with all the latent devilishness of his nature to unseat the man from his saddle.

"You have missed the great thing, *alors*, though you have been up here two years," he said. "You do not feel, you do not know. What good have you done? Who has got on his knees and changed his life because of you? Who has told his beads or longed for the mass because of you? Tell me, who has ever said, 'You have showed me how to live'? Even the women, though they cry sometimes when you sing-song the prayers, go on just the same when the little 'Bless you' is over. Why? Most of them know a better thing than you tell them. Here is the truth: you are little—eh, so very little. You never lied—direct; you never stole the waters that are sweet; you never knew the big dreams that came with

wine in the dead of night; you never swore at
your own soul, and heard it laugh back at you;
you never put your face in the breast of a woman
— no, do not look so wild at me! — you never
had — a child; you never saw the world and yourself through the doors of life. You never have
said, ' I am tired, I am sick of all, I have seen it all.'
You have never felt what comes after — understanding. *Chut*, your talk is for children — and
missionaries. You are a prophet without a call,
you are a leader without a man to lead, you are
less than a child up here. For here the children
feel a peace in their blood when the stars come
out, and a joy in their brains when the dawn
comes up and reaches a yellow hand to the Pole,
and the west wind shouts at them. Holy Mother,
we in the far north, we feel things, for all the
great souls of the dead are up there at the Pole in
the Pleasant Land, and we have seen the Scarlet
Hunter and the Kimash Hills. You have seen
nothing. You have only heard, and because, like
a child, you have never sinned, you come and
preach to us!"

The night was folding down fast, all the stars
were shooting out into their places, and in the
North the white lights of the Aurora were flying

to and fro. Pierre had spoken with a slow force and precision, yet, as he went on, his eyes almost became fixed on those shifting lights, and a deep look came into them, as he was moved by his own eloquence. Never in his life had he made so long a speech at once. He paused, and then said suddenly, "Come, let us run."

He broke into a long sliding trot, and Sherburne did the same. With their arms gathered to their sides, they ran for quite two miles without a word, until the heavy breathing of the minister brought Pierre up suddenly.

"You do not run well," he said; "you do not run with the whole body. You know so little. Did you ever think how much such men as Jean Criveau know? The earth they read like a book, the sky like an animal's ways, and a man's face like—the Writing on the Wall."

"Like the Writing on the Wall," said Sherburne, musing, for under the other's influence his petulance was gone. He knew that he was not a part of this life, that he was ignorant of it; of, indeed, all that was vital in it and in men and women.

"I think you began this too soon. You should have waited, then you might have done good.

But here we are wiser than you. You have no message — no real message to give us; down in your heart you are not even sure of yourself."

Sherburne sighed. " I 'm of no use," he said, " I 'll get out. I 'm no good at all."

Pierre's eyes glistened. He remembered how, the day before, this youth had said hot words about his card-playing, had called him — in effect — a thief, had treated him as an inferior, as became one who was of St. Augustine's, Canterbury.

" It is the great thing to be free," Pierre said, " that no man shall look for this or that of you. Just to do as far as you feel, as far as you are sure, that is the thing. In this you are not sure — no. *Hein*, is it not ? "

Sherburne did not answer. Anger, distrust, wretchedness, the spirit of the alien, loneliness, were alive in him. The magnetism of this deep, penetrating man, possessed of a devil, was on him, and in spite of every reasonable instinct, he turned to him for companionship.

" It 's been a failure," he burst out, " and I 'm sick of it — sick of it ; but I can't give it up."

Pierre said nothing. They had come to what seemed a vast semicircle of ice and snow, a huge amphitheatre in the plains. It was wonderful:

a great round wall on which the Northern Lights
played, into which the stars peered. It was opened
towards the North, and in one side was a fissure
shaped like a Gothic arch. Pierre pointed to it,
and they did not speak till they had passed through
it, and stood inside. Like great seats the steppes
of snow ranged round, and in the centre was a
kind of plateau of ice, as it might seem a stage or
an altar. To the North there was a great opening, the lost arc of the circle, through which the
mystery of the Pole swept in and out, or brooded
there where no man may question it. Pierre
stood and looked. Time and again he had been
here, and had asked the same question: Who
had ever sat on those frozen benches, and looked
down at the drama on that stage below? Who
played the parts? Was it a farce or a sacrifice?
To him had been given the sorrow of imagination,
and he wondered, and wondered. Or did they
come still — those Strange People, whoever they
were — and watch ghostly gladiators at their deadly
sport? If they came, when was it? Perhaps
they were there now unseen. In spite of himself
he shuddered. Who was the Keeper of the
House?

Through his mind there ran — pregnant to him

The Red Patrol

for the first time — a *chanson* of the Scarlet Hunter, the Red Patrol, the sentinel of the North, who guarded the sleepers in the Kimash Hills against the time they should awake and possess the land once more; the friend of the lost, the lover of the vagabond, and all who had no home : —

> Strangers come to the outer walls —
> (*Why do the Sleepers stir ?*)
> Strangers enter the Judgment House —
> (*Why do the Sleepers sigh ?*)
> Slow they rise in their judgment seats,
> Sieve and measure the naked souls,
> Then with a blessing return to sleep —
> (*Quiet the Judgment House.*)
> Lone and sick are the vagrant souls —
> (*When shall the world come home ?*)

He reflected the words, and a feeling of awe came over him, for he had been in the White Valley and had seen the Scarlet Hunter. But there came at once also a sinister desire — to play a game for this man's life-work here. He knew that the other was ready for any wild move; there was upon him the sense of failure and disgust; he was acted on by the magic of the night, the terrible delight of the scene, and that might be turned to advantage.

The Red Patrol

Pierre said : " Am I not right ? There is something in the world greater than the creeds and the
book of the mass. To be free, and to enjoy ; that
is the thing. Never before have you felt what
you feel here now. And I will show you more.
I will teach you how to know, I will lead you
through all the North and make you to understand the things of life. Then, when you have
known, you can return if you will. But now —
see ; I will tell you what I will do: here on this
great platform we will play a game of cards.
There is a man whose life I can ruin. If you
win, I promise to leave him safe, and to go out of
the Far North for ever, to go back to Quebec " —
he had a kind of gaming fever in his veins ; —
" if I win, you give up the Church, leaving behind
the Prayer-book, the Bible, and all, coming with
me to do what I shall tell you for the passing of
twelve moons. It is a great stake — will you play
it ? Come " — he leaned forward, looking into
the other's face — " will you play it ? They drew
lots — those people in the Bible ; we will draw
lots and see, eh ? and see ? "

" I 'll do it," said Sherburne, with a little gasp.
" I accept the stake."

Without a word they went upon that platform,

118

shaped like an altar, and Pierre at once drew out a
pack of cards, shuffling them with his mittened
hands. Then he knelt down, and said, as he laid
out the cards one by one till there were thirty,
" Whoever gets the ace of hearts first wins —
hein ? "

Sherburne nodded and knelt also. The cards
lay backs upwards in three rows. For a moment
neither stirred. The white metallic stars saw it,
the small crescent moon beheld it, and the wide
awe of night made it strange and dreadful. Once
or twice Sherburne looked round as though he felt
others present, and once Pierre looked out to the
wide portals as though he saw some one entering.
But there was nothing to the eye — nothing.
Presently Pierre said, " Begin."

The other drew a card, then Pierre drew one,
then the other, then Pierre again; and so on.
How slow the game was ! Neither hurried, but
both, kneeling, looked and looked at the cards long
before drawing and turning it over. The stake
was weighty, and Pierre loved the game more than
he cared about the stake. Sherburne cared nothing
about the game, but all his soul seemed set upon
the hazard. There was not a sound out of the
night, nothing stirring but the Spirit of the North.

Twenty, twenty-five cards were drawn, and then Pierre paused.

"In a minute all will be settled," he said. "Will you go on? or will you pause?"

But Sherburne had got the madness of chance in his veins now, and he said, "Quick, quick, go on!"

Pierre drew; but the great card held back. Sherburne drew, then Pierre again. There were three left. Sherburne's face was as white as the snow around him. His mouth was open, and a little white cloud of frosted breath came out. His hand hungered for the card, drew back, then seized it. A moan broke from him. Then Pierre with a little weird laugh reached out and turned over — the ace of hearts!

They both stood up. Pierre put the cards in his pocket. "You have lost," he said.

Sherburne threw back his head with a reckless laugh. The laugh seemed to echo and echo through the amphitheatre, and then from the frozen seats, the hillocks of ice and snow, there was a long low sound as of sorrow, and a voice came after:

"*Sleep — sleep. Blessed be the just and the keepers of vows.*"

The Red Patrol

Sherburne stood shaking as if he had seen a host of spirits. His eyes on the great seats of judgment, he said to Pierre: "See, see, how they sit there, gray and cold and awful."

But Pierre shook his head. "There is nothing," he said, "nothing;" yet he knew that Sherburne was looking upon the Men of Judgment of the Kimash Hills, the Sleepers. And he looked round, half-fearfully, for if here were those great children of the ages, where was the Keeper of the House, the Red Patrol?

Even as he thought, a figure in scarlet with a noble face and a high pride of bearing stood before them, not far away. Sherburne clutched his arm, and Pierre muttered an *ave*.

Then the Red Patrol, the Scarlet Hunter, spoke: "Why have you sinned your sins and broken your vows within our House of Judgment? Know ye not that in the new springtime of the world ye shall be outcast, because ye have called the sleepers to judgment before their time? But I am the hunter of the lost. Go you," he said to Sherburne, pointing, "where a sick man lies in a hut in the Shikam Valley. In his soul, find thine own again." Then to Pierre: "For thee, thou shalt know the desert and the storm and the Lonely Hills — thou shalt neither seek nor find. Go, and return no more."

The two men, Sherburne falteringly, stepped down, and moved to the open plain. They turned at the great entrance, and looked back. Where they had stood there rested on his long bow the Red Patrol. He raised it, and a flaming arrow flew through the sky towards the South. They followed its course and when they looked back a little afterwards the great Judgment House was empty, and the whole North was silent as the Sleepers.

At dawn they came to the hut in the Shikam Valley, and there they found a trapper dying. He had sinned greatly, and he could not die without some one to show him how, and to tell him what to say to the Angel of the Cross Roads; and his Indian guide knew only the password to the Lodge of the Great Fires.

But Sherburne, kneeling by him, felt his own new soul moved by a holy fire, and first praying for himself, he said to the sick man: " *For if we confess our sins, He is faithful and just to forgive us our sins, and to cleanse us from all unrighteousness.*"

And praying for both, his heart grew strong, and he heard the sick man say ere he journeyed forth to the Cross Roads: "You have shown me the way. I have peace."

"Speak for me in the Presence," said Sherburne softly.

The dying man could not answer, but as he journeyed forth that moment, he held Sherburne's hand.

The House with the
Broken Shutter

He stands in the porch of the world —
 (*Why should the door be shut ?*)
The gray wolf waits at his heel,
 (*Why is the window barred ?*)
Wild is the trail from the Kimash Hills,
The blight has fallen on bush and tree,
The choking earth has swallowed the streams,
Hungry and cold is the Red Patrol :
 (*Why should the door be shut ?*)
The Scarlet Hunter has come to bide —
 (*Why is the window barred ?*)

PIERRE stopped to listen. The voice singing
was clear and soft, yet strong — a *mezzo-
soprano* without any culture save that of practice
and native taste. It had a singular charm — a
sweet, fantastic sincerity. He stood still and fastened his eyes on the house, a few rods away. It
stood on a knoll perching above Fort Ste. Anne.
Years had passed since Pierre had visited the Fort,

The House with the Broken Shutter

and he was now on his way to it again, after
many wanderings. The house had stood here
in the old days, and he remembered it very well,
for against it John Marcey, the Company's man,
was shot by Stroke Laforce, of the Mounted
Police, the Riders of the Plains. Looking now,
he saw that the shutter, which had been pulled
off to bear the body away, was hanging there just
as he had placed it, with seven of its slats broken
and a dark stain in one corner. Something more
of John Marcey than memory attached to that
shutter. His eyes dwelt on it long — he recalled
the scene: a night with stars and no moon, a
huge bonfire to light the Indians, at their dance,
and Marcey, Laforce, and many others there,
among whom was Lucille, the little daughter of
Gyng the Factor. Marcey and Laforce were
only boys then, neither yet twenty-three, and they
were friendly rivals with the sweet little coquette,
who gave her favors with a singular impartiality
and justice. Once Marcey had given her a gold
spoon. Laforce responded with a tiny, fretted
silver basket. Laforce was delighted to see her
carrying her basket — till she opened it and showed
the spoon inside. There were many mock quar-
rels, in one of which Marcey sent her a letter by

The House with the Broken Shutter

the Company's courier, covered with great seals, saying, " I return you the hairpin, the egg-shell, and the white wolf's tooth. Go to your Laforce, or whatever his ridiculous name may be."

In this way the pretty game ran on, the little golden-haired, golden-faced, golden-voiced child dancing so gayly in their hearts, but nestling in them too, after her wilful fashion, until the serious thing came — the tragedy.

On the mad night when all ended, she was in the gayest, the most elf-like spirits. All went well until Marcey dug a hole in the ground, put a stone in it, and, burying it, said it was Laforce's heart. Then Laforce pretended to ventriloquize, and mocked Marcey's slight stutter. That was the beginning of the trouble, and Lucille, like any lady of the world, troubled at Laforce's unkindness, tried to smooth things over — tried very gravely. But the playful rivalry of many months changed its composition suddenly as through some delicate yet powerful chemical action, and the savage in both men broke out suddenly. Where motives and emotions are few they are the more vital, their action is the more violent. No one knew quite what the two young men said to each other, but presently, while the Indian dance was on, they drew to the side of the house, and had their duel out in the half-shadows, no one knowing, till the shots rang on the night, and John Marcey, without a cry, sprang into the air and fell face upwards, shot through the heart.

· They tried to take the child away, but she would not go; and when they carried Marcey on the shutter she followed close by, resisting her father's wishes and commands. And just before they made a prisoner of Laforce, she said to him very quietly — so like a woman she was — " I will give you back the basket, and the riding-whip, and the other things, and I will never forgive you — never — no, never ! "

Stroke Laforce had given himself up, had himself ridden to Winnipeg, a thousand miles, and told his story. Then the sergeant's stripes had been stripped from his arm, he had been tried, and on his own statement had got twelve years' imprisonment. Ten years had passed since then — since Marcey was put away in his grave, since Pierre left Fort Ste. Anne, and he had not seen it or Lucille in all that time. But he knew that Gyng was dead, and that his widow and her child had gone south or east somewhere; of Laforce after his sentence he had never heard.

The House with the Broken Shutter

He stood looking at the house from the shade of the solitary pine-tree near it, recalling every incident of that fatal night. He had the gift of looking at a thing in its true proportions, perhaps because he had little emotion and a strong brain, or perhaps because early in life his emotions were rationalized. Presently he heard the voice again: —

> He waits at the threshold stone —
>   (*Why should the key-hole rust ?*)
> The eagle broods at his side,
>   (*Why should the blind be drawn ?*)
> Long has he watched, and far has he called —
> The lonely sentinel of the North —
> " Who goes there ? " to the wandering soul :
> Heavy of heart is the Red Patrol —
>   (*Why should the key-hole rust ?*)
> The Scarlet Hunter is sick for home,
>   (*Why should the blind be drawn ?*)

Now he recognized the voice. Its golden *timbre* brought back a young girl's golden face and golden hair. It was summer, and the window with the broken shutter was open. He was about to go to it, when a door of the house opened, and a girl appeared. She was tall, with rich, yellow hair falling loosely about her head; she had a strong, finely cut chin and a broad brow, under which a pair of deep blue eyes shone — violet blue, rare and fine. She stood looking down at the Fort for a few moments, unaware of Pierre's presence. But presently she saw him leaning against the tree, and she started as from a spirit.

"Monsieur!" she said — "Pierre!" and stepped forward again from the doorway.

He came to her, and "Ah, *p'tite* Lucille," he said, "you remember me, eh? — and yet so many years ago!"

"But you remember me," she answered, "and I have changed so much!"

"It is the man who should remember, the woman may forget if she will."

Pierre did not mean to pay a compliment; he was merely thinking.

She made a little gesture of deprecation. "I was a child," she said.

Pierre lifted a shoulder slightly. "What matter? It is sex that I mean. What difference to me — five, or forty, or ninety? It is all sex. It is only lovers, the hunters of fireflies, that think of age — *mais oui!* "

She had a way of looking at you before she spoke, as though she were trying to find what she actually thought. She was one after Pierre's own heart, and he knew it; but just here he wondered where all that ancient coquetry was gone, for there were no traces of it left; she was steady of eye, reposeful, rich in form and face, and yet not occupied with herself. He had only seen her for a minute or so, yet he was sure that what she was just now she was always, or nearly so, for the habits of a life leave their mark, and show through every phase of emotion and incident whether it be light or grave.

"I think I understand you," she said. "I think I always did a little, from the time you stayed with Grah the idiot at Fort o' God, and fought the Indians when the others left. Only — men said bad things of you, and my father did not like you, and you spoke so little to me ever. Yet I mind how you used to sit and watch me, and I also mind when you rode the man down who stole my pony, and brought them both back."

Pierre smiled — he was pleased at this. "Ah, my young friend," he said, "I do not forget that either, for though he had shaved my ear with a bullet, you would not have him handed over to the Riders of the Plains — such a tender heart!"

Her eyes suddenly grew wide. She was childlike in her amazement, indeed, childlike in all ways, for she was very sincere. It was her great

130

advantage to live where nothing was required of her but truth, she had not suffered that sickness, social artifice.

"I never knew," she said, "that he had shot at you — never! You did not tell that."

"There is a time for everything — the time for that was not till now."

"What could I have done then?"

"You might have left it to me. I am not so pious that I can't be merciful to the sinner. But this man — this Brickney — was a vile scoundrel always, and I wanted him locked up. I would have shot him myself, but I was tired of doing the duty of the law. Yes, yes," he added, as he saw her smile a little. "It is so. I have love for justice, even I, Pretty Pierre. Why not justice on myself? Ha! The law does not its duty. And maybe some day I shall have to do its work on myself. Some are coaxed out of life, some are kicked out, and some open the doors quietly for themselves, and go a-hunting Outside."

"They used to talk as if one ought to fear you," she said, "but" — she looked him straight in the eyes — "but maybe that's because you've never hid any badness."

"It is no matter, anyhow," he answered. "I

131

live ·in the open, I walk in the open road, and I stand by what I do to the open law and the gospel. It is my whim — every man to his own saddle ! "

" It is ten years," she said abruptly.

" Ten years less five days," he answered as sententiously.

" Come inside," she said quietly, and turned to the door.

Without a word he turned also, but instead of going direct to the door came and touched the broken shutter and the dark stain on one corner with a delicate forefinger. Out of the corner of his eye he could see her on the doorstep, looking intently.

He spoke as if to himself: " It has not been touched since then — no. It was hardly big enough for him, so his legs hung over. Ah, yes, ten years — Abroad, John Marcey ! " Then, as if still musing, he turned to the girl: " He had no father or mother — no one, of course ; so that it was n't so bad after all. If you 've lived with the tongue in the last hole of the buckle as you 've gone, what matter when you go ! *C'est égal* — it is all the same ! "

Her face had become pale as he spoke, but no

132

muscle stirred; only her eyes filled with a deeper color, and her hand closed tightly on the door-jamb. "Come in, Pierre," she said, and entered. He followed her. "My mother is at the Fort," she added, "but she will be back soon."

She placed two chairs not far from the open door. They sat, and Pierre slowly rolled a cigarette and lighted it.

"How long have you lived here?" he asked presently.

"It is seven years since we came first," she replied. "After that night they said the place was haunted, and no one would live in it, but when my father died my mother and I came for three years. Then we went east, and again came back, and here we have been."

"The shutter?" Pierre asked.

They needed few explanations — their minds were moving with the same thought.

"I would not have it changed, and of course no one cared to touch it. So it has hung there."

"As I placed it ten years ago," he said.

They both became silent for a time, and at last he said: "Marcey had no one, — Sergeant Laforce a mother."

The House with the Broken Shutter

" It killed his mother," she whispered, looking into the white sunlight. She was noting how it was flashed from the bark of the birch-trees near the Fort.

" His mother died," she added again, quietly. " It killed her — the gaol for him ! "

" An eye for an eye," he responded.

" Do you think that evens John Marcey's death ? " she sighed.

" As far as Marcey 's concerned," he answered. " Laforce has his own reckoning besides."

" It was not a murder," she urged.

" It was a fair fight," he replied firmly, " and Laforce shot straight." He was trying to think why she lived here, why the broken shutter still hung there, why the matter had settled so deeply on her. He remembered the song she was singing, the legend of the Scarlet Hunter, the fabled Savior of the North.

> Heavy of heart is the Red Patrol —
> (*Why should the key-hole rust ?*)
> The Scarlet Hunter is sick for home,
> (*Why should the blind be drawn ?*)

He repeated the words, lingering on them. He loved to come at the truth of things by allusive, far-off reflections, rather than by the sharp ques-

The House with the Broken Shutter

tioning of the witness-box. He had imagination, refinement in such things. A light dawned on him as he spoke the words — all became clear. She sang of the Scarlet Hunter, but she meant some one else! That was it —

> Hungry and cold is the Red Patrol —
> (*Why should the door be shut ?*)
> The Scarlet Hunter has come to bide,
> (*Why is the window barred ?*

But why did she live here? To get used to a thought, to have it so near her, that if the man — if Laforce himself came, she would have herself schooled to endure the shadow and the misery of it all? Ah, that was it! The little girl, who had seen her big lover killed, who had said she would never forgive the other, who had sent him back the fretted-silver basket, the riding-whip, and other things, had kept the criminal in her mind all these years; had, out of her childish coquetry, grown into — what? As a child she had been wise for her years — almost too wise. What had happened? She had probably felt sorrow for Laforce at first, and afterwards had shown active sympathy, and at last — no, he felt that she had not quite forgiven him, that, whatever was, she had not hidden the criminal in her heart. But why did she sing that song? Her heart was pleading for him — for the criminal. Had she and her mother gone to Winnipeg to be near Laforce, to comfort him? Was Laforce free now, and was she unwilling? It was so strange that she should thus have carried on her childhood into her womanhood. But he guessed her — she had imagination.

"His mother died in my arms in Winnipeg," she said abruptly at last. "I'm glad I was some comfort to her. You see, it all came through me — I was so young and spoiled and silly — John Marcey's death, her death, and his long years in prison. Even then I knew better than to set the one against the other. Must a child not be responsible? I was — I am!"

"And so you punish yourself?"

"It was terrible for me — even as a child. I said that I could never forgive, but when his mother died, blessing me, I did. Then there came something else!"

"You saw him, *chère amie?*"

"I saw him — so changed, so quiet, so much older — all gray at the temples. At first I lived here that I might get used to the thought of the thing — to learn to bear it; and afterwards that

I might learn — " she paused, looking in half-doubt at Pierre.

"It is safe ; I am silent," he said.

"That I might learn to bear — him," she continued.

"Is he still — " Pierre paused.

She spoke up quickly. "Oh no, he has been free two years."

"Where is he now ? "

"I don't know." She waited for a minute, then said again, "I don't know. When he was free, he came to me, but I — I could not. He thought, too, that because he had been in gaol, that I would n't — be his wife. He did n't think enough of himself, he did n't urge anything. And I was n't ready — no — no — no — how could I be ! I did n't care so much about the gaol, but he had killed John Marcey. The gaol — what was that to me ! There was no real shame in it unless he had done a mean thing. He had been wicked — not mean. Killing is awful, but not shameful. Think — the difference — if he had been a thief ! "

Pierre nodded. "Then some one should have killed him ! " he said. "Well, after ? "

"After — after — ah, he went away for a year. Then he came back ; but no, I was always thinking of that night I walked behind John Marcey's body to the Fort. So he went away again, and we came here, and here we have lived."

" He has not come here ? "

" No; once from the far north he sent me a letter by an Indian, saying that he was going with a half-breed to search for a hunting party, an English gentleman and two men who were lost. The name of one of the men was Brickney."

Pierre stopped short in a long whiffing of smoke. "Holy !" he said, " that thief Brickney again ! He would steal the broad road to hell if he could carry it. He once stole the quarters from a dead man's eyes. *Mon Dieu!* to save Brickney's life, the courage to do that ! — like sticking your face in the mire and eating — but, pshaw ! — go on, *p'tite* Lucille."

" There is no more. I never heard again."

" How long was that ago ? "

" Nine months or more."

" Nothing has been heard of any of them ? "

" Nothing at all. The Englishman belonged to the Hudson's Bay Company, but they have heard nothing down here at Fort Ste. Anne."

" If he saves the Company's man, that will make up the man he lost for them, eh — you think that, eh? Pierre's eyes had a curious ironical light.

"I do not care for the Company," she said. "John Marcey's life was his own."

"Good!" he added quickly, and his eyes admired her. "That is the thing. Then, do not forget that Marcey took his life in his hands himself, that he would have killed Laforce if Laforce had n't killed him."

"I know, I know," she said, "but I should have felt the same if John Marcey had killed Stroke Laforce."

"It is a pity to throw your life away," he ventured. He said this for a purpose. He did not think she was throwing it away.

She was watching a little knot of horsemen coming over a swell of the prairie far off. She withdrew her eyes and fixed them on Pierre. "Do you throw your life away if you do what is the only thing you are told to do?"

She placed her hand on her heart — that had been her one guide.

Pierre got to his feet, came over, and touched her on the shoulder.

"You have the great secret," he said quietly. "The thing may be all wrong to others, but if it's right to yourself — that's it — *mais oui!* If he comes," he added — " if he comes back, think of him as well as Marcey. Marcey is *sleeping* — what does it matter? If he is *awake*, he has better times, for he was a man to make another world sociable. Think of Laforce, for he has his life to live, and he is a man to make this world sociable.

> The Scarlet Hunter is sick for home —
> (*Why should the door be shut ?*)

Her eyes had been following the group of horsemen on the plains. She again fixed them on Pierre, and stood up.

" It is a beautiful legend — that," she said.

" But ? — but ? — " he asked.

She would not answer him. " You will come again," she said; " you will — help me."

" Surely, *p'tite* Lucille, surely, I will come! But to help — ah, that would sound funny to the Missionary at the Fort and to others."

" You understand life," she said, " and I can speak to you."

" It's more to you to understand you than to be good, eh ? "

" I guess it's more to any woman," she answered.

The House with the Broken Shutter

They both passed out of the house. She turned towards the broken shutter. Then their eyes met. A sad little smile hovered at her lips.

"What is the use?" she said, and her eyes fastened on the horsemen.

He knew now that she would never shudder again at the sight of it, or at the remembrance of Marcey's death.

"But he *will* come," was the reply to her, and her smile almost settled and stayed.

They parted, and as he went down the hill he saw far over, coming up, a woman in black, who walked as if she carried a great weight. "Every shot that kills ricochets," he said to himself:

"His mother dead — her mother so!"

He passed into the Fort, renewing acquaintances in the Company's store, and twenty minutes after he was one to greet the horsemen that Lucille had seen coming over the hills. They were five, and one had to be helped from his horse. It was Stroke Laforce, who had been found near dead at the Metal River by a party of men exploring in the north.

He had rescued the Englishman and his party, but within a day of the finding the Englishman died, leaving him his watch, a ring, and a cheque

The House with the Broken Shutter

on the H. B. C. at Winnipeg. He and the two
survivors, one of whom was Brickney, started
south. One night Brickney robbed him and
made to get away, and on his seizing the thief
he was wounded. Then the other man came to
his help and shot Brickney: after that weeks of
wandering, and at last rescue and Fort Ste. Anne.

A half-hour after this Pierre left Laforce on
the crest of the hill above the Fort, and did not
turn to go down till he had seen the other pass
within the house with the broken shutter. And
later he saw a little bonfire on the hill. The
next evening he came to the house again himself.
Lucille rose to meet him.

"'*Why should the door be shut?*'" he said
smiling.

"The door is open," she answered quickly and
with a quiet joy.

He turned to the motion of her hand, and saw
Laforce asleep on a couch.

Soon afterwards, as he passed from the house,
he turned towards the window. The broken
shutter was gone.

He knew now the meaning of the bon-fire the
night before.

Lightning Source UK Ltd.
Milton Keynes UK
UKHW022016080321
380016UK00005B/842